A NOVEL BASED ON THE LIFE OF
NICCOLÒ MACHIAVELLI

THE MAKING OF A
PRINCE

Maurizio Marmorstein

THE MENTORIS
PROJECT

The Making of a Prince is a work of fiction. Some incidents, dialogue, and characters are products of the author's imagination and are not to be construed as real. Where real-life historical figures appear, the situations, incidents, and dialogue concerning those persons are based on or inspired by actual events. In all other respects, any resemblance to actual persons, living or dead, events, or locales is entirely coincidental.

Barbera Foundation, Inc.
P.O. Box 1019
Temple City, CA 91780

More information at www.mentorisproject.org

ISBN: 978-1-947431-17-1

Library of Congress Control Number: 2018907723

All net proceeds from the sale of this book will be donated to Barbera Foundation, Inc. whose mission is to support educational initiatives that foster an appreciation of history and culture to encourage and inspire young people to create a stronger future.

The Mentoris Project is a series of novels and biographies about the lives of great Italians and Italian-Americans: men and women who have changed history through their contributions as scientists, inventors, explorers, thinkers, and creators. The Barbera Foundation sponsors this series in the hope that, like a mentor, each book will inspire the reader to discover how she or he can make a positive contribution to society.

Contents

Foreword   i

Introduction   1513: Life in Exile   1

Chapter One   1478: School Days   9

Chapter Two   1513: Communing with the Ancients   21

Chapter Three   1478: Street Smarts   29

Chapter Four   1513: Sneaking Back into Florence   41

Chapter Five   1478: Conspiracy   53

Chapter Six   1513: The Dedication   69

Chapter Seven   1494: University Years   83

Chapter Eight   1513: Old Friends and Courtesans   97

Chapter Nine   1494: Sticks of Chalk   105

Chapter Ten   1513: *The Prince* vs. *Discourses*   117

Chapter Eleven   1498: The Second Chancery   129

Chapter Twelve   1513: My Little Book   145

Chapter Thirteen   1499: The Lady of Forlì   157

Chapter Fourteen   1513: "One's Own Arms and Ability"   177

Chapter Fifteen   1512: The Fall of the Republic   197

Chapter Sixteen   1513–1527: The Final Years   207

Acknowledgments   223

About the Author   227

Foreword

First and foremost, Mentor was a person. We tend to think of the word *mentor* as a noun (a mentor) or a verb (to mentor), but there is a very human dimension embedded in the term. Mentor appears in Homer's *Odyssey* as the old friend entrusted to care for Odysseus's household and his son Telemachus during the Trojan War. When years pass and Telemachus sets out to search for his missing father, the goddess Athena assumes the form of Mentor to accompany him. The human being welcomes a human form for counsel. From its very origins, becoming a mentor is a transcendent act; it carries with it something of the holy.

The Barbera Foundation's Mentoris Project sets out on an Athena-like mission: We hope the books that form this series will be an inspiration to all those who are seekers, to those of the twenty-first century who are on their own odysseys, trying to find enduring principles that will guide them to a spiritual home. The stories that comprise the series are all deeply human. These books dramatize the lives of great Italians and Italian-Americans whose stories bridge the ancient and the modern, taking many forms, just as Athena did, but always holding up a light for those living today.

Whether in novel form or traditional biography, these

books plumb the individual characters of our heroes' journeys. The power of storytelling has always been to envelop the reader in a vivid and continuous dream, and to forge a link with the subject. Our goal is for that link to guide the reader home with a new inspiration.

What is a mentor? A guide, a moral compass, an inspiration. A friend who points you toward true north. We hope that the Mentoris Project will become that friend, and it will help us all transcend our daily lives with something that can only be called holy.

—Robert J. Barbera, President, Barbera Foundation
—Ken LaZebnik, Editor, The Mentoris Project

Introduction

The memory of prison plagued him, and the torture he endured during those brutal days of winter just one short year ago settled deep into his bones. Niccolò Machiavelli had spent the last fourteen years working as chief ambassador for the Republic of Florence. He loved his native city above all else, and served it well. But all that came to an abrupt halt when the authorities showed up at his door, dragged him from his home, and threw him in prison without so much as a word of explanation. His interrogators showed little mercy. They jerked his hands behind his back, fastened them to chains linked to pulleys, and hoisted him into the air with savage indifference. It was a well-known and rather effective form of torture: the *strappado,* they called it. Florentines knew it as the *corda,* and would often gather in the Piazza della Signoria to witness common crooks and conspirators fall victim to it. The snap of Niccolò's shoulders failed to arouse any feelings in his interrogators. All in a day's work. The pain consumed him, eclipsed only by his anger, resentment, and the unrequited knowledge he was innocent of the charge they levied against him. Only when he drifted into unconsciousness could he hope to ever escape the torment of it. But they made sure to keep him awake at all times, splashing him with water if necessary.

Niccolò had certainly been aware of the cruelties committed in Florence's most infamous prison, the Bargello, while serving as secretary of the Second Chancery for the Republic, and he no doubt witnessed a traitor or two undergoing much of the same treatment, but now he knew of its inhumanity and powers of persuasion firsthand. He could hardly be accused of being averse to such methods, however. Far from it. The state and the security of its people ranked supreme in his eyes. In fact, he firmly held that the state and its institutions had a sacred duty to preserve their powers, especially when it came to ensuring the freedom of its people. Every broken bone, crack, fracture, and dislocated joint he suffered reminded him of that very belief. As he hung there, his wrists bleeding beneath the ropes that hoisted him high above the chamber's hard granite floor, the bitter irony of that belief nearly brought a smile to his lips.

On an unusually cold afternoon that following December, just nine months after his release from custody, Niccolò sat in his study in his country home in Sant'Andrea in Percussina with those gruesome, not-so-distant memories still swirling around in his head. They ran on a seemingly endless loop. A daily occurrence. Truth be told, Niccolò rarely dwelt on the past. His slender frame, medium height, close-set eyes, and aquiline nose gave the misleading impression of an inconsequential man, unconcerned with the world around him, but his sharp, hawk-ish eyes saw the present with eerie precision, and could divine the future like no other. His tight mouth and thin lips saddled him with an almost permanent sarcastic expression that managed both to command respect and lend an air of levity to his persona. His friends and colleagues in the Signoria, the city's center of government in the Palazzo Vecchio, held him up as a man of action, of unstoppable vigor and determination, invaluable to their efforts to keep the city safe and free.

But in the autumn of 1512, when the Republic fell back into the hands of the Medici, matters were about to change for the worse. The Medici, Florence's long-established family of bankers, were as ruthless as they were generous and forward-thinking, and as eager for the cold control over the masses as for the attainment of knowledge and beauty. They had already ruled over Florence prior to 1494, and it must be said that during that time their spiritual, intellectual, and financial support for the arts proved the envy of all Europe, but the Florentines desired freedom, a government run by the people. After the ouster of the Medici in 1494, a free Republic was installed, and for the next fourteen years Florence enjoyed democratic rule.

Niccolò's loyalty to the old, "free" Republic marked him as suspect almost immediately to the incoming rulers. It was no secret that he preferred the will of the people above all else. He was known to say that the people desired their own freedom, nothing more, nothing less. "It is in the interest of the aristocracy and members of the ruling class," he would go on to say, "to strip it away from them." Plain and simple. Those who knew him understood he wasn't advocating rebellion with those words as much as voicing a political truth he had gleaned from a lifetime of acute observation of human behavior and many years of experience as an ambassador for the Florentine Republic. As far as he was concerned, the sooner aspiring princes, tyrants, and kings understood that truth, the better.

Niccolò cherished these quiet moments alone in his study. They soothed him and put him at ease. He looked up from the manuscript on his desk—his "little book," he called it—and scanned the four walls teeming with classic tomes. Many of these books followed him from his youth on via Guicciardini, a stone's throw from the Ponte Vecchio and Piazza della Signoria, to his country home on Florence's hilly outskirts where he lived in exile with his family. He liked to converse with all the many authors as if they were sitting right there with him in that cold, drafty room, body and soul: Aristotle, Plato, Cicero, Ovid, Thucydides, Plutarch, Tacitus, Virgil, Dante, Boccaccio, Petrarch, and, of course, his two steady companions, Livy and Lucretius. He addressed them as equals, but with reverence, and oh so much urgency.

"I walked out of the Bargello a free man," he uttered to no one in particular as he rose to stoke the fire, hoping to remove the stubborn chill from the room. "Those blundering conspirators got what they deserved," Niccolò muttered, scorning the men with whom he was accused of plotting a revolt. "Let them die." He brooked no tolerance for their display of incompetence. "Oh, let them die!" he was heard shouting from his prison cell as the conspirators ascended the executioner's block. "Their foolishness has caused nothing but anguish for the innocent!"

Niccolò knew full well that while nothing endangered the survival of a ruler more than courtly intrigue—not even war itself—no enterprise could be more foolhardy and statistically futile. "How dare they accuse me of such an infamy!" He also knew that any failed attempt to topple the Medici's nascent government would provide more than enough pretense for their tyranny. Being a man of uncompromising practicality and stark realism, Niccolò easily grasped the self-serving logic of the powerful. He accepted it as fact. And he had precious little time for artless neophytes and would-be insurgents. Their failure always resulted in death and inevitably prolonged the suffering of the guiltless.

The massive window in Niccolò's study looked out onto row after row of Chianti grapes. He had visited this piece of family land nearly every summer since his birth forty-four years ago. The tiny hamlet of Sant'Andrea in Percussina sat fourteen kilometers southwest of Florence. He always wondered as a boy why the house was nicknamed the Albergaccio, or "bad hotel," and assumed it was due to the abundance of scoundrels and villains that roamed the nearby hills. He loved coming here just the same. Everything about it smelled of freedom. He particularly enjoyed running through the spot of woods beyond the vineyard, sprinkled with fir, ash, and pine. But he saw none of its beauty now. His thoughts drifted elsewhere as he fixed his gaze over the wooded hills that flanked his vineyard. In the nine months since his exile, since the end of the tragic war that toppled the Republic, these sparse woods had been a modest source of income, and he depended on them almost entirely for the sale of firewood. A meager existence. He fed his four children and dear wife, Marietta Corsini, with these sparse earnings, but even these harsh realities remained far from his mind at this moment. His thoughts instead swirled with concerns of the political state of his beloved city and of the entire Italian peninsula. He was burdened with far too much insight into the pangs of the human condition, and far too much desire to remedy it.

Niccolò was a city animal; life within the peace and tranquility of the Tuscan countryside terrified him. The notion of leading what he believed to be a pointless existence, wasting away to nothing in a puddle of country serenity, literally kept him awake at night. The taverns, government halls, town squares, and park benches of Florence met his needs, satisfied his intellect, and fed his soul. The steady exchange of ideas in a city rife with ideas was his life's blood. A sense of uselessness, emptiness, taunted him now, day in and day out. Meditating in his study, reading and rereading his books, communing as it were with ancient historians, recalling his many personal experiences as Florence's ambassador, and diligently writing down all his thoughts, political, personal, and otherwise, would have to fill that void.

As he glimpsed the encroaching night sky, Niccolò's musings kept returning to his many years as Florence's ambassador to the kingdoms of France, Spain, Naples, the Holy Roman Empire, and his neighboring Italian city-states, including the Vatican. He needed desperately to write it all down, to make practical use of his experiences, and to save them for the benefit of others. The title page of a short treatise on his desk caught his eye. He had written a first draft in a flurry of creativity over the past few weeks. The ideas and principles he brought to light within its pages filled him with a mixture of hope, pride, and sheer dread.

"I must be useful," he whispered to himself as he dipped his plume into a brimming well of iron gall ink. "I must be useful."

But before Niccolò did anything else, he knew he had an urgent letter to write, some thoughts he had to get off his chest. His friend and longtime colleague during his glory days as secretary of the Second Chancery, Francesco Vettori, had recently written to him from Rome grumbling of the sheer boredom of life in the Vatican. The papal city's obsession with decorum, formality, and unwavering convention drove him crazy. The predictability of it all tormented him, he wrote. Niccolò, who was not one to be outdone, felt compelled to teach his dear friend the real meaning of boredom, and to share with him a bit of the frustration that followed him from his prison cell to his oppressively tranquil and uneventful exile in the country. And, of course, as a way of saying "Niccolò shall always prevail," he fully intended to share the news of his new book with him, a treatise as steeped in traditional rhetoric as it was in truly original and provocative insight. Its title was straightforward and clear: *De Principatibus*—literally, *Of Principalities*. But it was often referred to simply as *The Prince* because it laid the groundwork for becoming a powerful, respected, and feared ruler of a sovereign state while articulating in no uncertain terms how to acquire and maintain it, by any and all means necessary.

Chapter One

1478: SCHOOL DAYS

Niccolò was imbued with an interest in human behavior and its effect on political interaction as far back as he could remember. As he composed his letter to his dear friend, he thought back on his childhood in Florence, the city that would mold his character and shape his entire future.

Florentines ate, drank, and breathed politics. At the time of Niccolò's birth in 1469, the city was quite wealthy and at the vanguard of western civilization in terms of cultural achievement. A rebirth in classical thought had been blooming there since the mid-1300s, with the likes of such literary and political giants as Petrarch, Boccaccio, Coluccio Salutati, and countless others. For them and numerous other scholars of the fourteenth and fifteenth centuries, the ancient cultures and societies of Rome and Greece—their art, architecture, literature, and their innate faith in the integrity of the state—provided principal sources of inspiration for their city.

At the core of this return to the classics by Italian humanists was not necessarily an overwhelming thirst for knowledge, although it certainly fueled the curiosity of many, but rather the need to apply a new moral system that complemented the customs and mores of the powerful merchant class, which had risen to prominence in the affluent city-states of central and northern Italy. Niccolò could boast neither the upbringing of the rich merchant class nor of a Florentine noble. He hailed from an old Tuscan family that originated in the tiny commune of Montespertoli, twenty kilometers southwest of Florence, not far from the home he would occupy later in his life in Sant'Andrea in Percussina. The family also owned properties in the Santo Spirito section of Florence, where Niccolò was born and raised. No matter how astute his prowess in the political arena, or how extraordinary his expertise and understanding of it, his social status as a "commoner" would render it nearly impossible for him to ever hold high office. He accepted it as a political reality. What choice did he have? Although he could claim some noble blood going as far back as the twelfth century, especially among the Montespertoli members of the family, his branch of the Machiavelli tree was firmly rooted in much humbler soil. His father, Bernardo, a lawyer by profession, could have by no means been considered a wealthy man. However, the family was hardly in dire straits. Bernardo's wife, Bartolommea de' Nelli, a pious woman from a well-established Florentine family, in all probability possessed a certain degree of culture given the simple fact that she could read and write. She composed poetic verses of respectable quality, all religious in nature, and all dedicated to the Virgin Mother. She and Bernardo were married in 1458. Their bond produced four children: Niccolò's two older sisters, Primavera and Margherita, and a younger brother, Totto.

One day in particular always stood out in Niccolò's recollection of his early years in his home on via Guicciardini. The year was 1478, and young Niccolò was approaching his ninth birthday. Primavera and Margherita, thirteen and ten years old, respectively, and four-year-old Totto were helping their mother in the kitchen as she prepared holiday cakes sweetened with candied fruit, nuts, and honey for the upcoming Easter season. Bartolommea was hardly alone in that endeavor. Every woman worthy to be called a true Florentine took great pride in the city's gastronomic customs, and therefore every dinner table within miles of the Arno river, the muddy waterway that coursed through the city, showcased the obligatory *Torta di Pasqua.* Tradition was not to be ignored. This did not mean, however, that the task of making sure Niccolò got to his Latin lessons on time fell by the wayside.

"Niccolò, Niccolò, come here!" she shouted. "You mustn't be late."

Bartolommea pulled two florins from her tapestry-embroidered purse. Niccolò came running, carrying a brand-new leather satchel over his shoulder stuffed with a copy of Cicero's *De Re Publica,* a leaden stylus, and a sheet of crude parchment. Bartolommea unstrapped her son's bag and slipped in several slices of fresh unsalted bread, followed by a wedge of fresh *casciotta,* the local sheep's cheese, and a handful of dried black olives from their grove in Sant'Andrea.

"And Ser Batista is to get every florin," she reminded him as she sealed the coins inside. Ser Battista di Filippo da Poppi had recently taken over for Master Matteo as Niccolò's Latin tutor.

His mother's voice grew solemn, and her cadence slowed considerably as she locked eyes with her young son. "And go straight to your lesson."

Niccolò knew what was coming next. He'd heard it a hundred times.

"And there's no stopping to chat with those blowhards by the bridge. Do you hear me? They will warp that delicate mind of yours beyond repair."

"But they speak of great men in our history, men who helped build our city," Niccolò said respectfully. "Their words ring as true and as close to my heart as the sermons I endure from Ser Battista."

"He is Florence's finest tutor," she shot back.

"His knowledge of books has no limit, it is true, and I am grateful. But there are those who have lived through much of our history, it is a part of them, and their words are like poems to me."

"Your father doesn't labor day and night to fill our shelves with fine books so you can learn your truths from the mouths of drunks. And I am no fool. You think I don't know they speak of women and nothing else? So much for your sweet poems! Now go, or Ser Battista will lock his doors to you. Go."

Niccolò smiled mischievously and scooted off.

The trip to Ser Battista's studio crossed the heart of the city. Niccolò ran as fast as he could through the crowds on the Ponte Vecchio, Florence's oldest bridge, now reserved for the city's finest jewelers and goldsmiths, and past the Porcellino market and the old drunks his mother had warned him about—although he made sure to slow down to catch a word or two of wisdom—and then hurried to the steps of the church of Santa Maria del Fiore, known to all Florentines as the Duomo. The front door of his tutor's studio was just a few meters down the road. Luckily, the key was still in the door.

Once Niccolò was inside, Ser Battista wasted no time in

chiding his young student. Teaching was his life, but patience hardly ranked as one of his virtues.

"Do you think I have all the time in the world for young fools like you? Let us get started."

Young Niccolò refused to be intimidated. He always came prepared. After only two years of Latin, he spoke it and wrote it as if he were Cicero himself.

Ser Battista relentlessly tested the boy's grammatical skills to root out his weaknesses, but the declensions rolled right off of Niccolò's tongue, and the fluency of his translations into his native Italian impressed his tutor to no end. Deep inside, Ser Battista thoroughly enjoyed passing on his knowledge to such a gifted pupil, but for the sake of principle he refused to show it. No student could ever presume to receive perfect marks.

"The highest praise is always reserved for God Himself," he often said. "And second place must go to the venerable professor," he added with a wry smile. "And, of course, the student naturally comes last in this hierarchy."

Despite all the discouragement and ridicule, Niccolò had discerned his tutor's deep respect for him from the first time he set foot in his studio, but rather than take advantage of the soft spot Ser Battista had for him by ignoring his studies as any normal young student might do, Niccolò reveled in peppering him with questions on Florence's heritage. No subject concerning the history of his beloved city was off limits. He especially enjoyed hearing of the great men who founded Florence's political institutions. Ser Battista obliged him without reserve. All of Florence's noted professors, officials, merchants, artisans, and even laborers believed that the best training in life, and in the political arena in particular, focused on the reading of ancient history and moral philosophy. Serving your country well, fighting tyranny and corruption, and holding values such as honor and glory were foremost in the minds of all Florence's citizens, young and old alike.

"Such enthusiasm for such a young boy!" his tutor happily declared as he prepared to deliver what Niccolò knew would be a longwinded but thoroughly illuminating lecture on the *studia humanitatis,* the humane discipline to which Florence had been committed since the rule of its first chancellor, Coluccio Salutati.

"Is it true that Salutati believed we are not under God's heavenly control?" Niccolò asked.

"Who filled you with such nonsense?" his tutor was quick to respond.

"You so much as said so yourself," answered Niccolò respectfully.

"The man was a passionate advocate of freedom. That is quite different," argued Ser Battista, "but he was a true believer of Our Lord Savior."

Young Niccolò thought for a moment. "Although God created the heavens and the world that surrounds us, and He has written our fate in the stars, in the end, living a moral life is our own responsibility," he said. Ser Battista suppressed a smile as Niccolò quickly continued, "God has given us the freedom to choose. This much I can see for myself."

Ser Battista took great pride in the budding wisdom of his students. A natural result of his teachings, he presumed.

"With freedom comes responsibility," he said. "If there is one thing you must always remember, young man, it is precisely that."

For a boy of nine, Niccolò felt uncharacteristically fascinated by something his peers routinely despised: responsibility. It was a concept his father, Bernardo, would often encourage in his children, and each time Niccolò would take his words to heart. He saw the benefits of it everywhere.

"Salutati felt a deep sense of civic duty," Ser Battista continued. "When he took hold of the reins of the government nearly a hundred years ago, our city and a good portion of our troubled peninsula were engaged in bloody conflicts. It is our curse!" he roared, working himself into a frenzy. "Salutati's calm words of diplomacy saved Florentine lives. He is a hero to the Republic."

Although Niccolò devoured every minute of his tutor's rolling discourses, he could hardly get a word in edgewise. For someone so full of questions, comments, observations, and opinions, it took every ounce of respect and patience Niccolò could muster to keep his mouth shut. He just sat back and listened. Ser Battista adored details and always began at the very beginning. He lauded Salutati's expert training in law at the prestigious University of Bologna and his break with the mindset of only applauding the contemplative life, so touted in earlier times. Salutati vigorously supported man's worldly activities such as politics and commerce. Following his election as secretary of the Florentine Republic in 1375, Salutati wasted no time in creating the conditions for the city of Florence to assume a leading role in the rebirth of classic thought and logic. These opening words, uttered so eloquently by Ser Battista, kept Niccolò's undivided interest, attesting to the boy's innate predilection for statecraft, but his ears really pricked up the moment his tutor broached the subject of Salutati's diplomatic skills.

Just like his new hero, Salutati, Niccolò loved to solve problems no matter what their nature. Niccolò was always driven by the desire to figure out how to anticipate possible conflicts and injustices. The old habits of relying on staid scholasticism to communicate abstract philosophical ideas held absolutely no charm for either Salutati or his young admirer. Niccolò enjoyed nothing more than captivating and persuading his young friends on via Guicciardini with the force of his well-chosen words. There could be no greater power, he thought, a notion that naturally drew him to emulate his Roman model, Cicero.

Salutati also realized that the written word had a seductive power all its own. When Ser Battista went on to explain how Salutati's style of writing, a natural blend of high and low verbal register, became a formidable mode of diplomacy and eventually set the standard for Florentine ambassadors for years to come, Niccolò's intuitive beliefs were confirmed.

"As the Republic grew increasingly embroiled in the bloody conflicts plaguing our peninsula," said Ser Battista, "the power of the pen rivaled that of the sword." Florence, in particular, he noted, rose to the occasion and promptly surged to the forefront of diplomacy and political propaganda.

Niccolò finally found a moment, a slight lull in Ser Battista's verbose lecture, to interject. "My father praises Leonardo Bruni as well. He called him our greatest chancellor."

"Your father grew up under Bruni's rule," Ser Battista replied with a smile, "as did I."

Niccolò sat back in his chair, surrendering to the can of worms he had just opened for his garrulous tutor who, as expected, rattled on in praise of how Bruni later refined what Salutati had so brilliantly started. Bruni took office as chancellor in 1427 and ruled intermittently until his death seventeen years later. It was evident that Bruni held a special place in Ser Battista's heart. His earlier oration on Salutati was thorough, but noticeably stiff, a bit distant, and scholarly. Salutati cut an important figure in Florentine history, and Ser Battista felt duty-bound to show the man a certain modicum of respect, but he had met Bruni in the flesh many years ago, so his level of enthusiasm rose dramatically upon the mention of his name. He shared many of Bruni's ideals and revered him as the precursor of philological studies. Talking about such a great man to his young pupil enlivened his spirit. Arms that rested calmly at his side during descriptions of Salutati's life now flailed and gesticulated without hesitation, and his cheeks blushed red with enthusiasm. Niccolò even detected the hint of a smile on his tutor's face, which of course Ser Battista did all in his power to hide.

"If you truly want to learn the history of our great city," Ser Battista said as he pulled a book from a sea of tomes that lined every inch of his studio walls, "I urge you to read this from cover to cover. Your grasp of Latin is quite sufficient, young man."

Niccolò's eyes lit up at the sight of the book his father had mentioned so often at the dinner table: *Historiarum Florentini populi*.

"It will accompany me everywhere," Niccolò replied as he bowed with respect, overjoyed to have received his tutor's vote of confidence. "And I shall read his every word."

Ser Battista's next reaction nearly sent the young pupil flying off his chair in surprise. It seemed his dour teacher had found something uproariously amusing in Niccolò's innocent words of appreciation. The man burst out laughing, and evidently couldn't stop. Niccolò had never witnessed such a spectacle within those hallowed walls. It was the kind of laughter that could easily be perceived as hysterical, the sound of a madman on the loose. Watching the body of an old, gray-haired professor thrash about so uncontrollably—his eyes spewing tears of pure joy—began to truly frighten the boy. *Has my distinguished tutor gone mad?* he wondered. *What could I have possibly said?*

"I shall read every word!" howled Ser Battista, his sides now splitting with unbridled laughter.

Niccolò's eyes remained fixed on him, following his every move. He had heard mention of Ser Battista's idiosyncratic ways—his days, even months, of uninterrupted solitude, alone in his room with books and papers stacked to the ceiling, with little to eat or drink. His father had warned him of the insanely difficult, convoluted, and cryptic questions Ser Battista would ask of his less-promising students, hoping to discourage them from ever setting foot in his studio again. His seemingly super-natural ability to recite Cicero's orations verbatim, in Latin, for hours on end were legend, but Niccolò had never heard of these intermittent fits of out-and-out guffawing and childlike giggling. All the boy could do was wait for the insanity to stop, which it eventually did, and quite abruptly, in fact. Niccolò just sat there, torn between his curiosity of what would come next and the fear of finding out.

The old Frankish hourglass that stood prominently on Ser Battista's oak desk released its last grains of sand. Ser Battista was a busy man and a new pupil stood waiting outside his door. It had already been well established in Niccolò's previous meetings with his tutor that he never exceeded his time limit. He therefore expected to either be kindly ordered to leave or receive a long-winded explanation of what had just transpired. At this point, both options seemed perfectly acceptable to the boy; leaving this madhouse would relieve him of the awkwardness that would surely follow, but he also knew enough about himself—despite being merely nine years old—that sooner or later, his insatiable curiosity would have to be satisfied.

It turned out to be sooner rather than later. Ser Battista pivoted in his chair and zeroed in on a series of tomes on his massive bookshelf, all roughly the same size and bound with identical cloth dust covers. He then tipped eleven more books off the shelf into his waiting hands, all in rapid succession, and piled them one on top of the other on his desk, forming a free-leaning monolith of sorts that wobbled ever so slightly, enough so that one false move or the faintest puff of wind would have them all come tumbling down. No one dared make a sound or move a finger. Time stood still. Niccolò had no choice but to wait for his tutor to break the ice.

Ser Battista placed the original book gingerly atop the other eleven, then sat staring at the precarious stack of tomes.

"*Historiarum Florentini populi*," he whispered with reverence. A moment later he added the words, "*libri XII.*"

Bruni's already-famous writings on the history of Florence came in twelve massive volumes. Bruni wrote without the yearning for the myth and romance of the previous centuries. He believed in a serious inquiry into the ancient world, an intensity of investigation that would lift Florence out of the shadows of the long, dark period that followed the collapse of the Roman Empire. He reached a level of thought that Ser Battista felt he could share with only a select few of his students. His piercing blue eyes fixed on the young boy sitting in front of him.

"Twelve volumes," he whispered in his native Florentine. "Are you still so arrogant that you can promise you will read every word?" Ser Battista tilted his head in Niccolò's direction, awaiting some sort of response.

Thirty-five years later, as Niccolò sat in his study about to compose a heartfelt letter to his dear colleague in Rome, he would recall this exact point in time as the beginning of his passion for history, his interest in great rulers and thinkers, the rule of law, and the institutions that go into making a just and sustainable sovereign state. He would remember with fondness how he accepted Ser Battista's daunting challenge with the simple words "*Sí, Maestro*."

Chapter Two

1513: COMMUNING WITH THE ANCIENTS

"*Magnificent Ambassador, I cannot tell you in this letter anything other than what my life is like right now, and if you should care to trade with me, I should be quite happy,*" wrote Niccolò. It pained him to pen those first few words to Vettori. He paused a moment to reflect. "*I am living on a farm,*" he continued, then paused once again.

"I am living on a farm," he repeated under his breath. Somehow he found the anguish of his days in prison at the mercy of his interrogators, and the unholy torture they inflicted upon him, as less of a humiliation than the tedium of his present existence. His life, as miserable as it was within the cold walls of the Bargello, brimmed over with purpose. As a respected member of the free Republic and a public servant, he felt proud to be an integral part of a government dedicated to serving its people. He accepted without reservation all of its inherent political dangers and deadly intrigues. Of course the new regime would accuse him of conspiracy, he reasoned, and hold him prisoner. He thought it only natural.

Niccolò ran the Second Chancery from 1498 to 1512. He oversaw all internal as well as foreign affairs, and served as the Republic's key ambassador for the highest-ranking government official, Chancellor Piero Soderini. Undergoing the pains of the *strappado* at the hands of the Medici government was practically considered a badge of honor. Each time they bound his arms behind him and hoisted him into the air, wrists snapping and shoulders popping from their joints, it reinforced the value of his fourteen years of service to the Florentine Republic. As peaceful and as wholesome as life was on the farm, and as rewarding as it was to live by the fruits of his labors, Niccolò couldn't shake the feeling that the world was passing him by. The thought of no longer making a difference haunted him.

"I get up before sunrise," he wrote, determined to convince Vettori that the dreariness of his Roman life could never compare with the tedium of the *Albergaccio*. *"I would then prepare some birdlime, load a stack of cages on my back, and venture outside in the hopes of catching a few thrushes."* This pastime, as pitiful and strange as it was, had thankfully gone by the wayside as winter progressed and birds migrated farther south. He would now go into the grove each morning and remain there for several hours to oversee the work of felling trees for firewood. Once there, he'd kill some time with the woodcutters, who always had a hard-luck story to tell about themselves or their neighbors.

Niccolò went on to describe all of his other daily activities with equal objectivity and distaste.

"After leaving the grove," he wrote, *"I would go to the inn across the way and converse with the locals about their worries, petty grievances, and life-long beliefs."*

Niccolò often admitted in private, however, that he enjoyed much of his time with the local farmers, artisans, and laborers who frequented the inn, regardless of their often-skewed opinions and misplaced convictions. This routine pastime represented his primary connection to the day-to-day happenings of the world. Rather than venture across the street to access the inn, not the most respectable of places, he would slip through the narrow underground alleyway that served as his wine cellar and enter the adjoining cantina leading to the inn's well-stocked kitchen. From there he would wander into the main room and join an ongoing card game. Taking this circuitous route helped him to maintain a certain amount of integrity among his neighbors and protect him from their idle, and often derogatory, chatter. *Better not to be seen entering a den of iniquity,* he thought to himself. After all, despite being regarded as a commoner while living in Florence, to the locals he was a landowner, a keeper of servants, and employer of day laborers, farmers, woodcutters, harvesters, and grape pickers. To them he was no doubt a man of respect. His time at the inn usually preceded a meager lunch hour with his family, which he described as a meal with *"such food as this poor farm of mine and my tiny property allow."*

Niccolò sat back in his chair to gather his thoughts. He shook his head in dismay and mused, *Today, of course, was no different.*

Once he consumed, digested, and slept off his midday meal, the next third of his day was a rehash of his earlier activities in the inn, which typically revolved around playing card games like *cricca* and a version of backgammon called *tric-trac* with the village butcher, miller, and furnace tender. Niccolò viewed this part of his routine with some ambivalence. It wasn't all gloomy; in fact, he thrived on it to a certain extent.

While living in Florence, he thoroughly enjoyed carousing with friends and colleagues until all hours. No tavern, street corner, or brothel was safe from the unrestrained merriment of Niccolò and his "gang," as they were known. Biagio Buonaccorsi was a loyal friend who remained at his side from early childhood and through his years at the Second Chancery. He and Niccolò were inseparable. His card games with Biagio and the locals never failed to provoke lively disputes, insults laced with choice profanity, and countless squabbles over money, right down to the penny. Biagio loved to argue about anything and everything, and Niccolò argued right back. He recounted all this to Vettori in his letter with a mixture of sarcasm and worldly pride.

"It keeps my brain from growing moldy, and it satisfies the malice of this fate of mine," he quipped.

After years as Florence's number one diplomat, waging hard-fought intellectual and psychological battles with formidable heads of state throughout Europe and the Italian peninsula, engaging in a few good old-fashioned brawls with the townspeople had its guilty pleasures. But it was how he spent his evenings that Niccolò wanted desperately to share with his dear friend in Rome.

Never one to wear his heart on his sleeve, but neither one to stifle true sentiment, Niccolò held back a tear as he began his next paragraph. He'd been through so much in the past year. As hardened as he was to the indifference and shameless cruelty of the world, especially the world of government and politics, he was, after all, made of flesh. His mask of stoicism and sophistication worked its magic in the public arena, before diplomats, ministers, heads of state, kings, cardinals, and popes, but within the four walls of this study, his inner sanctum, he freed his spirit of all restraint. He surrounded himself with books written by great minds, and felt no shame in conversing openly with them on the dire issues of state. He consulted with each of these men, all of them noble thinkers, gifted leaders, historians, and poets, as if they were ready and eager to share their hard-earned wisdom with him. It was a nightly meeting, and one that Niccolò cherished above all else.

In preparation for another book, still in progress, on the superiority of the republican form of government entitled *Discourses on the First Decade of Titus Livius,* Niccolò conferred nearly every evening, for months, with the ancient Roman historian Titus Livius. Livy, as he was called in the vernacular, was the author of *Ab Urbe Condita,* an exhaustive history of ancient Rome from its mythological founding by Aeneas after the fall of Troy to the city's actual beginnings in 753 B.C. on the Palatine hill to the rise of Augustus Caesar. Livy welcomed Niccolò into his circle with great affection. It was this intimate connection with Livy, and with all the ancients, that he wanted so desperately to share with his friend.

Niccolò leaned back over his desk to reread what he'd composed so far, making sure the letter effectively conveyed how his life had changed. He wanted his friend in Rome to absorb, in particular, the words he used to describe the last third of his day. Vettori had survived the Medici takeover and currently held an ambassador's post in the court of the new pope, Leo X, formally Giovanni de' Medici. Niccolò's purpose in maintaining communications with Vettori, however, extended beyond his friendship. First of all, he wanted to keep abreast of important matters of state with a knowledgeable insider, and second, he hoped to somehow slip back into the fold, perhaps with a small post within the new regime. A kind word or letter of reference from someone still rubbing elbows with those in command could make this happen.

Niccolò had written Vettori just two weeks earlier asking for some assistance in precisely this matter. In fact, Vettori figured prominently in Niccolò's ultimate plan to have his treatise, *The Prince,* delivered directly to members of the Medici family and eventually to the pope himself. Besides his desire to transmit his knowledge and unique insight garnered from his experiences as Florence's ambassador, Niccolò hoped to use his "little work" as a calling card of sorts for future employment within the Medici government. More than anything else, Niccolò needed to feel that he was being of service to the city of his birth, and ultimately to the entire Italian peninsula. In the bigger picture, he desired nothing more than to help mold the type of ruler that could find the courage and resourcefulness to rid Italy of the pangs of foreign invasion and occupation. The image of the prince he had described in his treatise was designed to do just that.

"On the coming of evening I return to my house and enter my study," he wrote. He glanced over at his dusty woolen cloak and grimy field boots in the corner of the room, then down at his crimson velvet housecoat and lambskin bedroom slippers. A smile crossed his lips, and he returned to his missive, satisfied.

"I then remove the day's clothing covered with mud and dust, and put on garments courtly and regal," he continued. *"Once appropriately attired, I enter the ancient court of ancient men, where I am received by them with great affection."*

Niccolò hesitated to jot down the next few words for fear of being thought insane.

"They speak to me," he whispered to himself. "I ask them the reason for their actions, and they kindly answer me."

He, of course, was not crazy. There was no saner man alive. He knew he was alone in that room and that no voices actually beckoned him. Yet he could hear them. Loud and clear. Their words revealed the wisdom of the ancient world. They provided the very oxygen Niccolò needed to survive within this luckless existence of his. For four peaceful hours each evening he forgot his troubles, the dread of poverty disappeared, and the fear of death no longer hovered over him. He was exactly where he belonged.

A rush of pure energy pulsed through Niccolò as he dipped his plume into the inkwell, anxious to dash off his closing words.

"I feed on that food which is mine, and for which I was born," he added with unabashed self-regard. *"And since Dante says it does not produce knowledge when we hear but do not remember, I have noted everything in my conversations with these great men in my little work,* The Prince, *where I debate what a princedom is, how it is acquired and sustained, and ultimately why it is lost."*

Niccolò felt confident that the fourteen years he had spent at the service of the Republic, his high-level diplomatic forays throughout the continent, and his knack for discerning human character had uniquely qualified him to discuss the art of the state. He hadn't necessarily written *The Prince* with the intention of showboating his political acumen or soliciting a job, but he hadn't been wasting his time during his tenure at the Second Chancery, either, and he was hell-bent on making that fact known.

"I shall dedicate this book to His Magnificence Giuliano Medici," he wrote, hoping that Vettori would act as his intermediary. As

the son of Lorenzo il Magnifico, the celebrated ruler of Florence throughout Niccolò's entire youth, Giuliano was a big fish in the Medici family. Niccolò swallowed a bit of his pride as he laid down the next sentence: *"It is my wish that our present Medici lords make use of me even if they begin by making me roll a stone."*

Niccolò's mood turned dark. He stopped writing for a moment to absorb the anger that surged within him. He let it color his thoughts and energize his words. After all, he'd been a responsible citizen his whole life, and honest to a fault. His dedication to his city, his government, and ultimately to his beleaguered country never wavered. Not a penny that didn't belong to him ever found its way into his coffers, despite the hundreds of opportunities, and despite the frequency and ease with which government officials almost uniformly would skim public funds. Niccolò was principled, upright, and trustworthy, and everyone knew it, even the new Medici lords who had him arrested for malfeasance. He scratched the final words of his letter in near rage.

"I have been honest and good for my whole life. And as a witness to my honesty and goodness I have my poverty!"

Chapter Three

1478: STREET SMARTS

Young Niccolò spent the entire week after his meeting with Ser Battista plowing through the first volume of Leonardo Bruni's *History of the Florentine People*. He couldn't get enough of it. The more he read about his cherished city, and about the Etruscans who settled it more than two thousand years earlier, the faster he read. The Etruscans eventually fled the plains on either side of the Arno for the hills several kilometers to the north for reasons of defense. The city in its present location began as an ancient Roman military outpost in 59 B.C. It started out as a settlement for soldiers loyal to Julius Caesar. They named their city Florentia, "the flower," which was later Italianized to become Florence.

The city of Niccolò's youth stood alone among its rivals on the Italian peninsula in its artistic beauty and the sheer elegance of its *palazzi,* churches, and town squares. But its charm and grandeur was offset by an unstable political infrastructure that allowed for only brief periods of harmony among a deeply divided populous. Despite a tradition of republican government that aspired to liberty and the noble ideals of Athenian democracy, bloody battles raged with uneasy regularity in Florence's streets; hostilities between feuding families, each with dreams of wielding its unchallenged hegemony over the city, carried on for centuries. At the same time, the political environment beyond the city's protective walls provided no less a threat to its security. The surrounding cities of Siena, Pisa, Pistoia, Prato, Livorno, Volterra, and Arezzo, which all eventually came under Florentine control, would at one period or another rebel against her authority.

The area outside Florence's sphere of influence presented a menacing picture as well. Intrigue, hostility, and ruthless ambition remained the rule of the day among powerful city-states such as Milan and Venice, the papal state in Rome, and the Kingdom of Naples, which included the entire southern portion of the peninsula and the island of Sicily. It's not difficult to imagine how tyrants and political strongmen could crop up so easily in such a weak and divided land where each state coveted and distrusted the other, and had recourse to neighbors and mighty allies on the continent to overpower its enemies. Florence lived under the constant threat of attack from both within and without. Conspiracies flourished, while at the same time a complex web of alliances between states gave rise to a cold and sophisticated system of international relations to secure a balance of power. With powerful states beyond the Alps such as France, Spain, England, and the Holy Roman Empire vying for a piece of the peninsula, each poised to strike, Florence knew that its freedom—an ideal its citizens held close to their hearts—could be extinguished at any given moment. Therefore, it had no choice but to become a key player on the European chessboard. Diplomacy and war became two sides of the same coin.

As he read, young Niccolò began to notice an alarming pattern in his city's long-embattled history: Despite living in this perpetual state of danger, the city continually refused to train a standing army to keep its enemies at bay. It relied instead on foreign militias and mercenaries to defend its liberty, which inevitably strained the government's financial resources, and more often than not left its citizens in the hands of untrustworthy and disloyal soldiers of fortune. The fact that Florence's affluent merchant class contributed heavily to this atmosphere of moral decline was not something Niccolò needed to read in a book; it was the mantra uttered by Florentines around every dinner table in its vast territory. Unfortunately, the people had become so accustomed to the comforts of wealth that they grew increasingly indifferent—or as Niccolò's father preferred to put it, more and more corrupt. As long as money circulated freely, Florentines went calmly about their business, leaving the sole responsibility of running the city and protecting it from its enemies to those in the Palazzo Vecchio.

Bruni's words made a lasting impression on the young boy. Having read only the first of the twelve volumes, Niccolò realized he had so much more to learn about the city of his birth and its inhabitants, which of course piqued his curiosity even further. He had to know what the old drunks who sat along the banks of the Oltrarno on his side of the river had to say. Just about everything he heard them utter was either unwittingly sustained by his tutor during one of his rants or by what he'd read in his father's private library. Some of these men worked for the Medici when Cosimo ruled the city. A few of them belonged to Florence's powerful wool guild in their younger years, while others worked as simple shopkeepers or laborers with years of worldly wisdom and practical experience behind them. Their passion for politics, a good bottle of wine, and a deck of Tuscan playing cards formed the common thread that bound these men together. They were Niccolò's teachers of choice and, yes, their digressions into the realm of women and affairs of the heart didn't hurt matters. He was, after all, quite a precocious little boy.

Fully aware that he was disregarding his mother's warnings, Niccolò snuck out of the house while she was gathering linens in the upstairs bedrooms to haul to the public laundry fountain. Since it was Holy Saturday, the day before Easter, his father had woken up early to travel into the country to conclude some family business. Niccolò, being the meticulous child that he was, and knowing he had to cover all his bases so as to not get caught, bribed his three siblings with large chunks of Easter bread to look the other way as he bolted down the stairs and out of sight. He ran the few hundred meters to the Ponte Vecchio in a flash.

A seedy *osteria* that had been in business since Giovanni Boccaccio frequented it more than a hundred years earlier sat diagonally across from the bridge's entrance. The burly owner would routinely place a few rickety tables and chairs outside the front door just before the midday meal to attract passersby, and on most days a select circle of old men would take advantage of that table to chat, play cards, and argue about the state of the world. A waiter would then come out with bowls of soup and a carafe of house Chianti to calm their nerves, slake their thirst, and curb their appetite.

When Niccolò showed up, the men had just started a round of *briscola,* an old card game that required shouting and lots of flagrant cheating to be played correctly. The game and its requirements were right up their alley. Fortunately, Niccolò found them in a contentious mood. Given the slightest bit of encouragement they could discuss anything and everything for hours. At first the boy hovered over each of them, noticing what cards they'd been dealt and taking note of how they played their hands, trying to learn a thing or two about the game. He dared not say a word, careful not to break their concentration or interrupt their schemes. No need to stoke their ire prematurely. The boy had a gift for knowing what to say and when to say it, and his knack for garnering all the information he wanted without anyone catching on was uncanny. It was a talent he inherited from his mother, who regularly applied appropriate doses of sweetness and persistence to get her way, and nearly always with the desired result. Niccolò watched his father fall victim to her premeditated charm offensive so many times that he'd learned to master the technique himself at quite an early age.

He therefore waited patiently until each player had won at least one round, and when emotions seemed even-tempered. No big winners, no big losers. However, he also knew he couldn't wait too long. He had to trigger a good solid debate before they generated one of their own.

Luckily, so far everything seemed to be playing out to Niccolò's advantage. Nothing during any of their matches provoked a heated discussion, no taxes had been levied lately, no wars had been declared, and no clergyman had behaved more than usually corrupt or depraved. They found nothing to complain about, although, truth be told, that had never hindered them in the past. And what's more, they had a full carafe of wine to soothe them and a warm April sun shining overhead. At least for these few moments of card playing, perched on the corner of Florence's oldest bridge, the Ponte Vecchio, life was sweet.

Finally seizing the moment, Niccolò declared, "My tutor has proclaimed that our Republic under Medici rule is the best in the history of the world."

"What tripe!" they howled in unison. The range of their voices achieved a scratchy harmony of sorts.

"A young rascal like you should have laughed in his face!" one of them shouted.

Another one patted Niccolò on the back, "If you believe your dear tutor's drivel, there is a cupola atop our magnificent Duomo I'd like to sell you."

After the laughter died down, the oldest and most respectable one in the crowd, most likely an ex-bureaucrat under the Bruni Chancellorship, peered straight into young Niccolò's eyes. "It can indeed be argued that education under the Medici has fostered the growth of literature, philosophy, and rhetoric, as well as the practical arts of accounting, oratory, and even the craft of letter writing," he said. "Your generation has been well informed regarding every topic under the sun, in great part thanks to Maestro Poggio Bracciolini's influence on Salutati and Bruni after him. They, of course, influenced Cosimo de' Medici, and now Lorenzo il Magnifico, but I'll wager that you, and those like you, have learned nothing that resembles the truth."

"You forgot to mention Cosimo's son and Lorenzo's doting father," interjected the osteria owner as he placed a crock of salted black olives on the table. He was referring to Piero de' Medici, who ran the family's affairs after his father's death in 1464. The owner dutifully proclaimed a toast as he filled everyone's cup with the house Chianti: "To Piero, the best Medici of the lot."

They all burst out laughing, downed their wine, and refilled their cups within seconds.

"God favored us all by inflicting him with a severe case of gout and a very brief run of the government," one quickly added.

"Five of the longest years of my life!" shot back another.

The youngest of the lot felt obliged to whisper "Long live Lorenzo" in honor of the Medici scion currently pulling the strings.

They raised their cups again, one and all.

"*Cin cin*," they mumbled, and chugged down their wine as if it were cool, fresh water from a mountain spring. A moment of silence followed as they licked their moustaches dry and replenished their cups.

The ex-bureaucrat finally broke the ice. "Medici, Albizzi, Strozzi, Pazzi, Tornabuoni—they are one and the same. Our illustriously greedy families are all the same."

"The smell of their decadence still lingers," said another as he shuffled the cards in anticipation of another match.

Their resignation to the current state of affairs was apparent. Niccolò knew he had to interject again, and fast, or lose the momentum. Before another intense round of briscola threatened to commandeer the conversation, he blurted: "What is the use of elections if one family holds the reins of the entire city?"

"Have you not been listening, boy?" barked the ex-bureaucrat. "We have traded our freedom for comfort and decadence."

"Here, here," emerged spontaneously from everyone's lips.

Niccolò could read body language like it was his mother tongue. He could tell that the energy of confrontation, the urge to debate world affairs, still hung in the air. The signs were everywhere: fingers pattering on the table, toes tapping the cobblestone, and eyes flitting left and right. It was just a matter of time before tempers erupted, arguments ensued, or opinions simply had to be vented. He just had to be patient.

"It started with Cosimo the Elder," said one, getting the ball rolling. "Leonardo Bruni had to put up with that man's hegemony for ten years."

The words "The beloved father of our country" slipped out sarcastically from several lips. "Our dear *pater patriae*."

"The price a state must pay for stability," retorted another, a tinge of irony in his voice.

"Once again, the fault of our warring families," cried the ex-bureaucrat in a clear reference to the clashes between the Medici and Albizzi families that forced Cosimo, then leader of the Medici family, to abandon the city in 1433, forty-five years ago. "They are all an effrontery to democracy."

The discussion gathered steam and ran the gamut of topics for the next hour, but it always came back to the rise of Medici power in the city. Regardless of Florence's complex and relatively well-oiled government machine, every citizen knew who really pulled the strings behind the scenes. Rome had its corrupt popes; Milan and many of Italy's northern city-states had its impetuous dukes and princes; Naples had its haughty Aragon kings; and Florence had the Medici. Unlike the rest of Europe, where the transfer of power was guaranteed through the bloodlines of its aristocratic class, offering its populous at least the veneer of stability, Italy's leaders were not necessarily of noble birth; their rise to dominance often came about by other means, usually less than peaceful. In this sense, the presence of the Medici family on the political scene, bankers by profession, provided a modicum of stability for the Florentine Republic. The Medici had held sway over the city since 1434 when, as a result of a popular uprising, Cosimo the Elder was called back into Florence after a year's exile. If Cosimo wielded a considerable amount of influence before his banishment, he went a long way toward solidifying it upon his return.

"He persecuted and exiled every remaining Albizzi foe he could get his hands on," said the ex-bureaucrat as he slammed a trump card onto the table to win the match.

The rest of the players tossed their remaining cards in the dealer's direction. They were geared up for another match, another liter of wine, and yet another round of Medici bashing.

"His takeover was bloodless; I'll say that for him," one of them added.

"But vicious," said another, who went on to describe Cosimo as a man who had little patience for those who denounced him as an excessively harsh and vengeful tyrant. To such criticism Cosimo often responded that a decisive leader must rule with a firm hand, and that a state could not, and should not, be governed with prayers, or *paternosters,* as he was wont to say. The interests of the city were of vital importance to Cosimo; everyone around the table agreed on that. But his concern for Florence's welfare was usually overshadowed by his own interests and those of the Medici family.

Niccolò couldn't have been happier to hear the free flow of opinions. This was the type of information he could glean from no teacher employed in a city under Medici rule, and certainly from no history book. Of particular interest to the boy was how such power could be attained, and sustained, within an ostensibly republican system.

"But if Cosimo the Elder was a private citizen with no official title in the government, how could his authority survive?" the boy asked.

The ex-bureaucrat smiled. "With creativity and audacity."

Everyone nodded in agreement.

"The Balía was his brainchild," he added. Seeing Niccolò's puzzled look, he explained, "It was a ruling committee created to elect chief magistrates that were beholden to Cosimo, and only to Cosimo."

"And this made him stronger?" inquired Niccolò, now completely caught up in the discussion.

As he peered around the table he could sense their growing respect for him. The tone of the conversation shifted from the usual ranting and raving of drunks to one of wise elders bequeathing their hard-earned knowledge to the next generation. They had often seen young Niccolò linger on the sidelines of their card games, and on occasion even noticed the intensity of his focus and concentration. They assumed he was only interested in picking up a few tips on how to cheat at briscola. After all, there was money to be made for those who could master this old pastime, and the sight of this boy, albeit a seemingly well-mannered Florentine youth, hanging around a seedy tavern naturally led them to presume the worst. They now could see he had a brain in his head.

"The Balía consolidated his power," the ex-bureaucrat affirmed. "They held office for five years."

"And everyone in the city accepted it?" asked Niccolò.

"Cosimo's sway over the Republic was secured without having to shed a single drop of blood," said the ex-bureaucrat.

"But of course he would resort to violence if necessary," the osteria owner chimed in as he refilled their carafe with fresh Chianti.

"He sidestepped laws when he had to, and compromised ethics where convenient, but he governed with *modi civili*," added the ex-bureaucrat, "which, I must say, has remained the Medici style even under Lorenzo il Magnifico's rule today."

Despite the ex-bureaucrat's disdain for Medici dominance and his obvious affection for a free and open republic, he felt he had to speak fairly and objectively in front of Niccolò. He was simply stating a common perception. Cosimo was a man of limited culture, a merchant by trade, but he quickly realized that in a modern society, art, science, and literature were valuable resources into which every government had to invest. He surrounded himself with learned men and talented artists; he built libraries, churches, and public buildings.

Lorenzo il Magnifico was continuing in that same tradition. He rose to power nine years ago, in 1469, the very year Niccolò was born. The men around the card table all agreed that Lorenzo's imposing figure and his inclination to take decisive action was forging a positive impression on the Florentine people, which no doubt rankled members of rival families, but which naturally consolidated Medici hegemony even further. Like his grandfather, Cosimo, and his father, Piero, who ruled for only a few years before him, Lorenzo assumed no official title in the government, but fully controlled what was ostensibly still a free republic.

"He lends money to growing businesses and gives important positions in government to his friends and allies," said the ex-bureaucrat.

"A loan to our small shop in Santo Spirito kept us from starving to death," admitted the dealer as he motioned to the player next to him to cut the deck.

"There is no denying he has helped many families in distress," the ex-bureaucrat agreed, "but his system of favors and cronyism only serves to mask his growing power over Bartolomeo Scala and the rest of the Signoria."

This last statement rang true to Niccolò, whose father, Bernardo, regarded Bartolomeo Scala, Florence's current chancellor, as a close friend. Bernardo was no stranger to the workings of government and may have easily enjoyed an inside track regarding affairs of state and Lorenzo il Magnifico's influence over them, which he openly shared with his family and relatives around the dinner table. Chances were better than even that Sunday gatherings at the Machiavelli residence consisted of a healthy portion of *ribollita* stew, home-baked unsalted bread, the family wine, and plenty of fresh gossip from the inner circles of town hall.

"What about Volterra?" cried the ex-bureaucrat.

"Lorenzo resorted to violence to expropriate its alum mines," added the dealer as he hurriedly issued three cards to each player to begin the match.

"Where do the city's interests begin and Medici interests end . . ." interjected Niccolò.

They all laughed.

"He's no fool," said the ex-bureaucrat. "When word of his victory circulated, we all poured into the streets to rejoice."

Niccolò was quick to respond. "That wasn't a question. I was merely being rhetorical."

The men laughed even louder, each one making sure to pat Niccolò on the back to demonstrate their approval.

"Rhetorical?" one chuckled. "Such a big word for such a little boy."

Chapter Four

1513: SNEAKING BACK INTO FLORENCE

As usually happened after a long night of working on his books or writing letters to friends and former colleagues, Niccolò woke up groggy and more than a little ruffled. He opened his bedroom window to breathe in the cold country air; threw on his breeches, shirt, and waistcoat; and went downstairs to eat a quick breakfast of stale bread and watered-down wine. After putting on his riding boots, lambskin coat, and thick woolen mantle, he grabbed his leather satchel from his study, slipped his letter to Vettori safely inside, and strode out the back door to his courtyard. Rather than venture out into the grove to meet his woodcutters, he hurried into the nearby shed to ready his horse for a trip to Florence.

He rarely visited his home on via Guicciardini since the family's big move into the country—he knew Medici eyes would be on him at all times—but the postal courier who routinely stopped by the inn to gather mail hadn't been seen for days, and getting his letter mailed in haste was top priority. Gianluca, the innkeeper, assured Niccolò that the courier's disappearance shouldn't be taken too seriously.

"He will show his face sooner or later," the innkeeper wheezed in his breathy Tuscan accent.

The mere words "sooner or later" always drove Niccolò crazy. It seemed to be everyone's answer for everything. After nine months in Sant'Andrea, he still couldn't get used to the local population's altered sense of time. Things didn't necessarily move slowly; when a job needed to get done, everything chugged along at a relatively steady pace. No one feared a hard day's work. Working, sleeping, and eating were what they did best. But when it came to events out of their control, they had the wisdom of Solomon and the patience of Job.

As far as virtues went, patience never ranked as one of Niccolò's strongest, a bad trait he more than likely picked up many years ago from his beloved but restless tutor, Ser Battista. God knows, Niccolò's composure and equanimity had been tested on more than one occasion during his many diplomatic missions on behalf of the Republic. Of the seven heavenly virtues prescribed by the Church, he could claim proficiency in only four: diligence, kindness, charity, and, on rare occasion, humility. He had little use for the remaining virtues of chastity, temperance, and, of course, patience. The four cardinal virtues of prudence, justice, fortitude, and temperance observed by the ancient Greeks and Romans were more to his liking, although once again the virtue of temperance eluded him. It wasn't that he didn't hold self-restraint in the highest regard; he realized its many benefits, but his appetite for life was simply too ravenous to control. Case in point—the real reason for traveling into the city on this brisk December morning extended far beyond wanting to post a simple letter. No, he possessed enough patience or self-restraint to wait for the courier to eventually arrive, but what truly motivated him was his craving to share a few liters of wine with old friends—especially Biagio—talk politics and women into the wee hours of the night, and cruise the narrow alleyways of the city looking for mischief.

Nine months of self-imposed exile from Florence also did much to stoke Niccolò's latent desire to be surrounded by beauty and art. For the first forty-three years of his life, Niccolò had occupied himself primarily with literature, history, politics, and philosophy. The many artists, and artistic wonders, that Florence nurtured didn't necessarily interest him any more than the average educated or cultured person. Of course, like all good Florentines he appreciated the many churches, monuments, piazzas, statues, paintings, and palazzos that embellished his beloved city, and like all good men of letters he could spend hours critiquing works of art and architecture with his sophisticated friends and colleagues, but for the most part his thoughts focused on the intrigues and complexities in the political realm.

Living in the Tuscan countryside, however, had heightened his yearning for the type of culture that only a modern city like Florence could provide. He never had to stray too far from home to visit the Brancacci Chapel in the Santa Maria del Carmine church, where Masaccio painted Adam and Eve's eviction from the Garden of Eden. The three-dimensional reality of the fresco was so innovative that it stunned the very young and impressionable Niccolò the first time he saw it. Masaccio's fresco of the Holy Trinity in Santa Maria Novella had much the same effect on him. As a boy he ran by Lorenzo Ghiberti's bronze panels on the doors of the Baptistery on his way to his Latin lessons, and, of course, he marveled at the Duomo, as did all the citizens of Florence. He no doubt stopped on more than one occasion to admire them, a habit that stuck with him throughout his adult life.

Of significant interest to Niccolò, however, was Brunelleschi's massive cupola atop the Duomo, a work of art in which every citizen of Florence took great pride. It was, after all, without question the largest and most beautiful freestanding dome in all the world. To live within sight of it connected Florentines to the heart of their city and tethered them to the soul of their homeland. They wore their proximity to the cupola, their view of it from their windows or balconies, the ability to see it each day, like a badge of honor. No one else on the Italian peninsula, or on the entire continent, could claim such brilliance. Their bond with the cupola felt almost spiritual, and Niccolò's link to it was no different. Having a view of it from his home in Sant'Andrea, a patch of land situated high up in the hills with a clear vista of Florence in the distance, left a bittersweet taste in his mouth. This "look but do not touch" relationship to his native city slowly tore him apart. To keep his sanity, every once in a while he just had to sneak in and see it up close.

But, of course, the cupola wasn't the only work of art that lured Niccolò back to the city. During his years at the Second Chancery, Niccolò met many young artists who were commissioned by the gonfalonier, Piero Soderini, to work in the city's public and private spheres, some of whom were Florentines of his same generation. Michelangelo Buonarotti, born in the heart of Florence and just six years younger than Niccolò, completed his most famous work to date, the statue of *David,* in the early years of Niccolò's tenure at the Chancery. Niccolò adored that statue. He passed by it almost daily in the Piazza della Signoria on his way to work. Of all the many pieces of art displayed within the city walls, it was this depiction of the young King David that Niccolò treasured most. It displayed strength in the face of overwhelming odds, a virtue Niccolò valued above all others, and reflected his penchant for the stylistic ideals of ancient Rome and Greece. The emphasis these two great empires placed on the glory of living in the "here and now," rather than looking to the afterlife for fulfillment, matched his temperament, as did their call for decisive action to resolve conflicts instead of relying on the strategy of appeasement so rigorously advanced by the Church of Rome. He saw religious figures of the ancient world, such as the young King David, sculpted in a classical style by local artists to be the perfect example of Florentine determination and assertiveness.

Sandro Botticelli, a native of the Ognissanti neighborhood of Florence just across the river from Niccolò's boyhood home, painted many religious works, but it was his classical subjects such as the *Birth of Venus* and *Primavera* that caught Niccolò's eye, as well as the attention of many art aficionados of the period, in particular the Medici. And just nine years earlier, in 1504, while working at the Chancery, Niccolò signed the contract for the noted painter, engineer, and inventor Leonardo da Vinci to paint a portrayal of *The Battle of Anghiari* in the council chamber of the Palazzo Vecchio, despite believing that battle to be a perfect example of Italy's declining military discipline. It was clear to Niccolò that the mercenaries who ran both armies in that fight had no allegiance to anyone, and therefore no real motive for success. He had read all about this famous Florentine victory in Anghiari waged seventy-five years ago against the far superior Milanese forces in Bruni's *History of the Florentine People* as a young boy, and undoubtedly felt a sense of pride at the time, but since formed a negative opinion of the whole event. Nonetheless, it ranked as one of Florence's greatest military accomplishments and deserved to be venerated.

It was cold and misty when Niccolò finally arrived in the center of Florence. Biagio, who knew nothing of his planned trip, was thrilled to see Niccolò's thin, tired face at his front door. It was close to lunchtime, and Niccolò wanted nothing more than to stroll the streets of the city, taking in some of the sights, and register his letter to Vettori with the postal service before finally sitting down to a hearty meal at the Osteria Casalinga in the Santo Spirito, just around the corner from his family home. Even though Biagio had visited Niccolò just a few days earlier, there was still plenty to talk about. They fed off each other's passion for world events, political gossip, and their obsession with airing their opinions on everything from how best to boil tripe to the sweetness of Petrarch's sonnets. These little reunions never failed to raise their blood pressure while also bringing them to an inevitable state of inebriation—it seemed they couldn't talk without consuming substantial quantities of local red wine. And, of course, there was never a shortage of good food to warm their bellies.

The owner and headwaiter, Alvaro, brought them both a basket of freshly baked bread and hot bowls of ribollita. Niccolò insisted on eating at the Casalinga because their recipe for this popular Tuscan vegetable stew matched his mother's almost to a T, and rivaled it in flavor. His poor mother, Bartolommea, had passed away in 1496 when he was only twenty-seven, and for all the years subsequent to her death he made it a point to dine at Casalinga's on special occasions. Of course, now that he lived in the Albergaccio, every visit to Florence qualified as a special occasion. He particularly liked the proportion of cannellini beans to the amount of fresh kale in the osteria's recipe, and their olive oil was always crisp, pungent, and just the right shade of translucent green. Niccolò's finicky taste buds served him well in his native Italy and on occasion at the court of Louis XII, but ruined just about every visit he ever made to parts of Spain, Switzerland, and the Hapsburg court in Austria. Biagio, on the other hand, didn't care what he ate as long as there was plenty of it.

"So what brings you to our fair city?" joked Biagio as he stirred his ribollita with a wooden spoon, checking for chunks of garlic-smeared bread to eat up first.

"My thirst for knowledge is insatiable," quipped Niccolò, "and what better place to drink of the cup of erudition than with an old friend?"

"What you mean to say is the Albergaccio is driving you mad," said Biagio. "Besides, erudition hasn't reared its noble head around here since poor Pico entered the gates of paradise."

"You speak nonsense as usual," shot back Niccolò, half serious. "The quest for knowledge has seeped into our bones since Petrarch and Boccaccio walked these very streets, to say nothing of Dante Alighieri. It is what makes us Florentines. Pico was a giant who stood on the shoulders of giants."

Pico della Mirandola, a man for whom both Niccolò and Biagio had tremendous admiration, stood uncontested as the greatest genius of their time, and a man of almost superhuman potential due to his extraordinary memory and proficiency in twenty-two languages including Latin, Greek, Arabic, and Hebrew. What made this feat so incredible was his premature death at only thirty-one years of age. Niccolò read Pico's book, *Oration on the Dignity of Man,* extolling the human quest for knowledge while he was still a student at the university. What struck him at the time was Pico's reversal of the traditional interpretation of Genesis held by the Church for centuries. According to the young author, eating from the tree of Good and Evil—that is to say, seeking knowledge—was not humanity's original sin and the cause of its downfall, but instead humanity's primary reason for being.

"It is a wonder he escaped the long arm of the Inquisition," said Biagio.

"He can thank il Magnifico for that," replied Niccolò.

"Do I hear you commend a Medici prince?" said Biagio sarcastically. "Have the wounds of humiliation and torture in the Bargello already begun to heal?"

"As you will see in my little book, I give praise where praise is due," Niccolò answered without batting an eye.

Biagio filled Niccolò's cup to the brim. "Drink. Perhaps it will bring you to your senses."

"Il Magnifico was many things, but he was not a simpleton," said Niccolò after gulping down a good portion of his wine. "He too was persuaded by Pico's argument that man's nature is neither moral nor immoral, that we are free to shape our lives as we so choose, and, above all, we must strive for perfection."

"I see you want to add excommunication as a heretic to your woes just as Pope Innocent VII did for poor Pico," said Biagio soberly. "To strive for perfection is to presume you will become like God. I assume you have heard of an angel called Lucifer, and what happened to him."

"I speak not of sinful pride, but of the search for the divine. It is our only path to salvation," said Niccolò, "and besides, after Pope Innocent's death, Pico was pardoned by dear ole Alexander VI the moment he donned his papal robes."

Biagio nearly fell off his chair from laughter. Alexander VI? Had country life softened his old friend's brain?

"Our dear ole Borgia pope was no simpleton, either," he said, "but he was a thief, a scoundrel, a philanderer, a degenerate, and the most corrupt Bishop of Rome we have ever known."

"You are absolutely correct," laughed Niccolò, "but as you know, I have a habit of giving praise where praise is due."

Biagio laughed right along with him. He missed Niccolò's intelligence, his rationality, and his sharp wit, but most of all he missed his friendship. They had spent many days working together, and many long nights carousing the streets of Florence. But the atmosphere had changed considerably since the Medici reared their tyrannical heads last year and put an end to the free Republic. Both men were out of favor within the new government, a fact that Biagio had learned to accept with a certain amount of dignity. Then again, Biagio never had Niccolò's passion for his job, nor his talent for diplomacy. It was precisely that passion and raw talent that the new regime lacked. Biagio knew it, Niccolò knew it, and they both suspected that the Medici lords knew it. Niccolò's disappointment over being spurned by the Medici was written all over his face, and Biagio had read it instantly upon seeing him at his front door, just as he had read it dozens of times before while visiting him at the Albergaccio. Being the good friend that he was, Biagio felt suddenly compelled to put an end to the levity, bring the conversation down to an emotional level, look his old friend in the eye, and talk straight.

"So, you still haven't answered my question," he said.

This brought a faint smile to Niccolò's face. Moments like these reinforced Niccolò's respect for Biagio as a man of profound awareness. He wasn't exactly sure what Biagio was alluding to, but Niccolò could see that he understood his underlying mood. Niccolò now knew the time was right to get down to the business at hand.

With that faint smile still pasted on his face, he asked facetiously, "And what question would that be, my friend?"

"I know you haven't come all this way just to post a letter," laughed Biagio, "and I won't presume to think you are here on my account."

Niccolò scooped up a spoonful of ribollita. He held it out in front of him, waving it every so often to emphasize his words.

"Peace will never come to us if we do not unite as a people," he said. "Our future and that of the entire peninsula relies on a strong, sustained, and courageous stand against the powers that threaten us. Freedom from foreign subjugation will forever elude us until we, the people of Italy, shed our differences and rally around a common goal, with common values, and spill our own blood, Italian blood, for those very values." His eyes fixed on Biagio's for a moment, then he disposed of his ribollita without missing a beat.

Biagio remained uncharacteristically silent, leaving room for Niccolò to add, "Only a man of virtue can forge the path to liberty; only a prince with the intelligence and insight to discern the current political realities, armed with the adequate resources and willing to use them to do whatever is necessary in pursuit of that liberty, can save us at this moment in time."

"Perhaps if you allow me to read that little book you so generously shared with others, I will be able to converse with you on equal footing," said Biagio with a touch of indignation. "I assume this exhortation to arms occupies a good number of its pages."

"Actually, it does not," Niccolò replied. "I hope to append a chapter on precisely that topic in the coming days. I had intended at first to dedicate the book to Giuliano de' Medici, and my letters to Vettori are a testament to that, but now I am having second thoughts."

"If I know you, my dear friend, that prince of which you speak so eloquently can only refer to one man, and that man's name is Niccolò Machiavelli."

"I would not be so bold as to presume such a thing," Niccolò shot back, betraying a smile, "but there is no denying that I just so happen to possess the learning and practical knowledge of such a man. Unfortunately, my lack of resources, political influence, and noble heritage preclude me from that role. No, my friend, my place is elsewhere."

"Where might that be?"

"Wherever I can be of use."

"And you hope this little book of yours will help?"

Niccolò gave a slight nod. "But first I would like to impose on your friendship and expertise, if I may, to peruse the words I have composed thus far before I commit them into the hands of our Medici lords."

Biagio couldn't contain his happiness. He nodded his consent and poured a healthy amount of wine for each of them in celebration.

Niccolò raised his cup. "There has been far too much division—too much infighting and conspiracy among our leaders."

Their cups met. "To freedom," they proclaimed in unison.

Chapter Five

1478: CONSPIRACY

The bells of every church and chapel in the city rang out in unison, calling the vast Florentine congregation to Easter mass. The Machiavellis were practitioners of Santo Spirito, a church for which they enjoyed a certain affinity due to its scholarly foundation nearly two hundred years earlier. Its convent doubled as a literary center for groups, led by Giovanni Boccaccio, the noted author of the *Decameron*—a book dear to the hearts of all Florentines, especially to young Niccolò's father, Bernardo, despite its infamously profane content. What further endeared Bernardo to the local parish was the library Boccaccio bequeathed to it, later frequented by the likes of Petrarch, Salutati, Bruni, and Cosimo de' Medici. Work to rebuild the church began shortly before Bernardo was born, and, in keeping with its foundation of celebrating classical ideals and principles, Brunelleschi, the architect responsible for the cupola atop the Duomo, presented a classical design for the church's interior in the form of a Latin cross with side chapels, and forty niches along its perimeter. On Sunday mornings while attending services with his family, Niccolò found himself marveling as much at the aesthetics of the church as at the ostentatious spectacle of high mass. This Easter morning was no different.

Even at the early age of nine Niccolò felt more attuned to the practical implications of religion than to its more spiritual offerings. His belief in God was no more nor less than that of his peers, but what he immediately noticed after weeks of religious training in preparation for his first Holy Communion was that the laws of God did as much to keep him in line as did the laws of man. In fact, violating the commandments promised greater peril for the guilty than the temporal penalties of the state. It seemed that these two institutions working in tandem made for greater overall stability, one complementing and reinforcing the other. Parish priests, bishops, cardinals, and popes wielded the same power, if not more, than officers of government. Sermons by the priest on the pulpit differed little from the orations of great leaders or men of influence, each with their own particular words of inspiration, and each with their dire warnings, rules, and strict laws for the general populous. These similarities and differences were brought into stark relief by the conversation he had the previous day with the old men by the Ponte Vecchio. Their words had a way of ruminating in his mind for days afterward.

"Niccolò, where is that head of yours?" scolded his mother as she knelt for the prayer of the Eucharist.

Niccolò snapped out of his reverie. Looking around, he suddenly realized that he was the lone person standing while the entire congregation had settled stoically onto the hard wooden kneelers. He quickly assumed the proper position and joined the liturgy in progress, but in the back of his mind he continued to ponder how institutions like the church and the government affected his life, and that of his family. Florence, its customs, traditions, and idiosyncrasies, were all he really knew of the world at his tender age. He had traveled with his mother and father to their home in Sant'Andrea and to the nearby town of San Casciano on numerous occasions, but life there wasn't much different in terms of people's basic beliefs and practices from life in the city, and, of course, being a part of the Florentine Republic they were subject to the same laws as all its citizens.

However, he intuitively knew that matters of state and religion could differ from region to region; his study of history, albeit limited given his age, reinforced that notion, as did his readings of those novellas in the *Decameron* that dealt specifically with travelers to foreign lands—of course, the novellas in the book having to do with the sexual misadventures of all the many clergymen and women, and naughty husbands and wives, were strictly off limits to the young boy. And, as always, the old men by the Ponte Vecchio, several of whom had visited the Levant and regions farther east as merchants in their youth, spoke vividly of their encounters with people of different religions, customs, and cultures. Niccolò also instinctually perceived religion, one's belief in God, to be quite different from the institution of the Church—that is to say, the complex system of tenets, rules, and regulations devised by a hierarchy of men to carry out the word of God. In this sense, he considered government and church to be quite similar. *People are people,* he thought to himself.

His tutor, Ser Battista, rarely spoke of political affairs in a partisan manner, especially current ones. In fact, he hardly discussed anything that even remotely dealt with everyday events. As a prudent man, he meticulously avoided any mention of the city's prominent families and influential men presently roaming the halls of the Signoria—and, of course, any critical reference to Lorenzo il Magnifico, or the Medici in general, was entirely taboo in public discourse, which was precisely what attracted Niccolò to the old men by the Ponte Vecchio! Ser Battista did, however, make a point of inculcating his young impressionable students with civic lessons. How the government functioned and what constituted a decent citizen were consistently part of his repertoire. This, too, fascinated Niccolò. His curiosity for discovering how things worked, especially in the realm of human organizational behavior, proved insatiable.

His two older sisters teased him relentlessly, calling him a nosey busybody. His mother was often moved to tears having to field all the many questions young Niccolò hurled her way, but deep inside Bartolommea cherished every torturous minute of it. His father learned to deal with him by providing as many books as possible to quench his thirst for knowledge, but there's no denying Bernardo also enjoyed sharing what he knew of the world with his inquisitive son. Parents know their children; they know every intimate feature of their personalities. Bartolommea and Bernardo had high hopes for their young busybody, and they couldn't have been prouder.

On this particular Easter Sunday, the church was filled to the brim with neighborhood families. Nearly every one of them rose from their pew to approach the altar rail when it came time to receive their Holy Communion. Bartolommea and Niccolò's sisters did the same. Not having gone to confession that morning, Bernardo thought it best to refrain from receiving the sacrament. Niccolò stayed behind with him, at least for the moment, to keep an eye on his younger brother, Totto. Taking advantage of the confusion caused by members of the congregation filing into the aisles and slowly caravanning toward the front of the church, Niccolò leaned over to ask his father a question.

"Can I speak to the Magnificent Gonfalonier Scala?" he whispered.

Bernardo reared back to think a second. He'd been caught off guard. The depth and scope of his son's questions never ceased to amaze him, but asking for a meeting with a former chief government officer of Florence took the cake.

"And just what would you like to say to him?" replied his father with a mixture of parental pride and natural Florentine sarcasm.

"How it all functions," answered Niccolò.

"How what functions?"

"Florence," the boy replied.

Like most young Florentines, Niccolò had heard about the workings of the government, its institutions, its bureaucracy, and its day-to-day activities from everyone except the people who were actually directly involved in it. This simply wasn't enough for someone of young Niccolò's spirit of inquiry. He knew what all educated citizens knew: that despite strong, often despotic leadership by the Medici, the city of Florence possessed a vibrant and complex republican infrastructure. At its core, the city was a free republic. The chief executive officer, or gonfalonier, held office for two years and ruled within prescribed parameters. He was required to be a member of one of the seven great guilds that oversaw the government, thus ensuring the predominance of the merchant class within the constitution and suppressing the old aristocracy that no longer held sway over the city. Financiers, industrialists, and businessmen, known as the *popolo grasso,* were the groups most notably represented, while the wool, cloth, and bankers' guilds actually managed to wield the most influence. Although members of these greater guilds maintained prominent positions within the institutions, the lesser guilds and day laborers, or *popolo minuto,* also maintained adequate levels of representation. A Council of Eight, known as *priori,* composed of six members of the greater guilds and two from the lesser guilds, collaborated with the gonfalonier to comprise the ruling Signoria, an old term understood as "lordly power" and used to distinguish itself from the old medieval Comune.

Niccolò was also quite aware, as were most educated boys in Florence at the time, that there were two houses of legislature: the *consiglio del comune,* or upper house, made up of members of the noble class; and the *consiglio del popolo,* or lower house, which possessed Florence's ultimate constitutional sanction of approving or disapproving all proposals sent to it by the Signoria. And then, of course, there was the Balía, the committee charged with appointing the city's magistrates, which everyone knew, although never openly admitted, compromised the city's true freedom by representing the not-so-subtle arm of Medici influence over the government.

"So you want to talk to our esteemed gonfalonier, do you?" asked Bernardo.

Niccolò locked eyes with his father. "I see no reason why he should refuse to speak to me," he said.

Bernardo betrayed a hint of a smile, which of course was not lost on the boy, who responded with a wide grin of his own. Their bond was strong, in particular over matters concerning young Niccolò's education. Bernardo was respected in the community as a studious and intelligent man. He kept a sort of diary in which he meticulously recorded family events as well as personal musings. He made it a point to document each new book he added to his home library, acquiring them by whatever means necessary. Sometimes he bought them, despite their often-prohibitive prices, or traded them for fresh food garnered from his land in the country. In order to nurture his healthy appetite for knowledge as well as that of his inquisitive young son, he often borrowed books from friends and colleagues. Cicero and Aristotle were his favorites. To indulge young Niccolò's love of history, he made sure to buy a copy of Livy's *History of Rome,* and anticipating his son's maturing interest in the condition of man, he negotiated a trade with a book vendor in the university district to acquire Titus Lucretius's majestic poem, *De Rerum Natura,* on the grand origins of nature.

"I see no reason why I shouldn't bring you to talk to our esteemed gonfalonier," said Bernardo, reaching down to caress his son's cheek. "He might learn a thing or two," he added with a smile. "Mother will hurry home after mass with Totto and the girls to prepare the lamb for the Easter meal, and we, in the meantime, shall pay a visit to an old friend."

Bartolommea and Bernardo parted ways the moment mass ended, she with her children minus Niccolò, and he with his son at his side. Niccolò led the way, hustling down the Borgo San Jacopo to the Ponte Vecchio. Bernardo quickened his pace to keep up.

"How can you be in such a hurry when you don't even know where you're going?" asked Bernardo.

Niccolò didn't bother to answer. He continued his march, determined to get wherever he was going as quickly as possible. A sumptuous lunch was scheduled to begin in two hours, and he wanted as much interaction with Gonfalonier Scala as time would allow.

As they crossed the bridge teeming with people going to

and from their church services, bells rang out in several nearby towers. The mood was festive at first, but as the clanging grew louder and spread to nearly every church steeple in the city, the din became deafening, which in turn brought on a good amount of confusion, followed by chaos, and finally sheer panic. People scrambled every which way. Some sought refuge indoors from the constant ringing, others simply covered their ears and quickened their gait hoping to outrun the commotion, but every one of them understood that the bells heralded bad news.

"What the devil is happening?" was the cry most heard.

Bernardo caught up to his son as they crossed the Ponte Vecchio, but Niccolò would not be deterred from his meeting with Gonfalonier Scala, no matter the circumstances. He ran even faster.

"Niccolò! Niccolò!" shouted Bernardo. "Stop!"

The boy did not relent.

"Stop!"

But it was no use. As Niccolò rounded the corner into Piazza della Signoria, Bernardo grabbed the boy's arm, finally bringing him to a halt. All the noise and the ensuing madness in the streets had chipped away at his patience. He spun young Niccolò around. The boy knew right then and there he had gone too far.

As he braced himself for the worst, the sound of galloping horses pounding against the cobblestone brought all action in the piazza to a standstill. Every man, woman, and child froze in place, gaping at the approaching cavalcade of black stallions, ten in all, rushing headlong down the via dei Calzaiuoli, the conduit connecting the Duomo to the Piazza della Signoria and ultimately to the seat of Florentine government in the Palazzo Vecchio. Strident cries of "Freedom!" from the men atop those horses rose above the cacophony of the bells, and grew increasing louder and more forceful as they poured into the piazza. Niccolò and his father stood in awe at the raw power and authority of the spectacle.

"Freedom, freedom!" the men continued to shout as they stopped in front of the Palazzo Vecchio, their clenched fists pumped high into the air. "Freedom!"

"I know him," said Bernardo, pointing to one of the men. "That is Jacopo Pazzi."

Niccolò didn't need any further explanation. Pazzi was the patriarch of a prestigious and influential banking family, and his name was familiar to everyone.

"Open the doors!" shouted Pazzi.

He dismounted, as did the other nine men. They bounded up the stairs to the massive front doors.

"Open up!" they ordered.

"Your time as tyrants of the city has ended!" cried the gentleman at Pazzi's side, his noble stature and authoritative tone distinguishing him above the rest. "As rightful archbishop of the city of Florence, I demand that you let us in at once!" The man unsheathed his sword, flailing it menacingly. "Medici rule has run its course!"

The metallic clanging of levers being unbolted from inside the palazzo gave way to some slight movement of the massive doors. For a moment it remained the only sound that could be heard. The tolling of the bells throughout the city persisted, and the distant cries of confusion and fear held constant, but the screeching of cast iron levers and locks captivated the entire piazza, dulling the sound of everything else around it. All eyes focused intently on the spectacle being played out on the steps of the city's most important building. Like the beginning of a grandiose Greek tragedy, a hushed anticipation accompanied the opening of the front doors.

Bernardo turned to his young son. "There is treachery in the air."

Pazzi whispered something to the nobleman wielding his sword, and bolted down the front steps to his horse, which he mounted in one clean, fluid leap, and galloped off.

"Who is that man?" asked Niccolò, pointing to the nobleman.

"Whoever he is will either be the next leader of our fair city—or a dead man," remarked Bernardo without taking his eyes off the doors, which suddenly threatened to screech wide open. "I'm afraid we shall know the answer to this question much sooner than we care to."

"That is the Archbishop of Pisa," cried a man standing directly behind Bernardo, "Francesco Salviati!"

The mere mention of his name caused a stir throughout the crowd. Murmurs buzzed through the piazza like a swarm of hornets. The anxiety was palpable. An apparent shakeup of Florence's internal affairs by a foreign figure signaled a great deal of trouble for the stability of the city. Shouts rang out among many in the crowd: "Cowards . . . cowards . . . cowards!" Others, spooked by the escalating gravity of the situation, backpedaled out of the piazza, expecting the worst.

Bernardo took his son by the hand. "Let us go, son. We have no place here."

Niccolò resisted. "It is one thing to read about historic events, but here they are taking place right before our eyes!"

"May I remind you that history is usually made up of war and death?" said Bernardo firmly. "We must leave at once."

The front doors of the palazzo finally spread wide, but no one came forth. From where Niccolò stood, he could discern the shadows of men standing deep inside the spacious Hall of the Five Hundred at the fore of the inner palazzo. The band of conspirators on the steps, led by the Archbishop of Pisa, rushed inside. The massive doors screeched shut behind them.

Everyone in the piazza stood motionless, waiting for something to occur. Anything. But nothing happened. No sound of conflict inside could be heard. No explanation of what had just transpired. Just silence.

As if awaking from a dream, Bernardo and Niccolò turned their attention from the palazzo to the crowd in the piazza and the incoming streets. The people stood paralyzed, craning their necks from side to side, from person to person, searching for answers. None came.

Just as everyone began to disperse, a grieving woman entered the piazza from via dei Calzaiuoli. "They have killed him!" she cried. "Poor Giuliano is dead!"

Another voice howled from behind her. "Il Magnifico has been assassinated . . . blood will run in the streets . . . run for your lives!"

After that, nothing could stop the flow of agitated citizens flocking into the piazza, all exclaiming the same message: The city was in open revolt.

Uncertain what chain of events would befall them and their beloved city, and fearing the worst, many in the crowd instinctively fled for more protected areas. Most returned to the safety of their homes. Watching such portentous events unfold right before his eyes, Niccolò had no intention of abandoning the scene. Bernardo was, of course, of a different mind. He grabbed his son's hand and steered him down the narrow alley to the Lungarno. There was no doubt in his mind they were going home.

The extended Machiavelli family gathered for lunch an hour

later. Bartolommea's mother and father, as well as Bernardo's brother and his wife and children, sat around a long oak table. Tension hovered over the room like a dense fog. Theories as to what exactly transpired that morning, and what it meant for the city, ran rampant. One piece of information, however, had been substantiated numerous times by eyewitnesses fleeing the scene of the crime, and therefore was held to be true: Lorenzo il Magnifico and his brother, Giuliano, were stabbed while attending high mass in the Duomo. Rumors that the Pazzi were behind the conspiracy appeared credible, especially given their rivalry with the Medici, and were corroborated by the sight of their patriarch, Jacopo Pazzi, at the Palazzo Vecchio.

"Whom do we stand behind?" asked Niccolò, "and whom will the people support?"

"Does it matter what we think?" said Bernardo cynically. "Yes, the Medici are tyrants, but we have done well under their tutelage. In the end, however, neither the Pazzi nor the Medici care a fig what any of us may think."

"I believe the Pazzi anticipated a show of support by the people to aid their cause," said Bernardo's younger brother. "Perhaps our little Niccolò here is right—it may be time to choose a side."

"And if we were to choose neither?" rejoined Niccolò mischievously.

The room fell silent. All eyes at the table turned to the boy. He saw the fear of uncertainty in those eyes as well as a glimmer of hope, as faint as it might be, for a truly free republic. No one there had ever lived without Medici rule, and therefore without the oversight of one of Florence's influential families. The thought of existing in that void—living truly free— was terrifying, but at the same time, it was a notion firmly embedded in the hopes and dreams of every Florentine citizen. No one ventured a direct response to Niccolò's provocation, but Bartolommea, who usually stayed clear of political discussions, offered a prognostication of sorts.

"Il Magnifico helped many families in despair," she said calmly. "The people will not want a change. Not yet."

"If it is true that il Magnifico is dead, then we may not have a choice," replied Bernardo.

"But why did they kill him?" cried little Margherita.

"And how do we know he is dead?" added her sister, Primavera, offering a ray of hope.

"We don't," said Bernardo, anxious to rekindle the spirits of his two young daughters. He then fixed his attention on everyone around the table. "But one thing is certain," he declared soberly, "no matter the outcome of today's events, change is coming. There is no turning back."

"Which is why we must say something," said Niccolò.

"*We* who?" inquired his father.

"The citizens of Florence," answered the boy without hesitation.

Ordinarily, his son's precociousness would fill Bernardo with pride, particularly during family events such as these, but lately the boy had been exhibiting the disturbing signs of being entirely too big for his britches. And what appeared to be even more galling, if not downright embarrassing to his father, was that the boy often made a lot of sense.

Bernardo demurred. "No matter what happens, I want everyone to stay in the house until we are sure our city is safe," he uttered without averting his gaze from Niccolò. "Is that clear?"

A rumbling in the street suddenly caught everyone's ear. Niccolò hurried to the window. His sisters followed, and as the distant ruckus gave way to chants of "Medici . . . Medici . . . Medici," the rest of the family jumped up from the table to witness the commotion outside. A line of people on via Guicciardini extended all the way down to the home of the banker Luca Pitti; this massive palazzo acquired by the Medici twenty years earlier now served as their family residence. The crowd seemed to be marching to the Ponte Vecchio and beyond, most likely to the Piazza della Signoria. More and more able bodies joined forces with the marchers as they passed by, and the chants in support of the Medici intensified. The citizenry had indeed chosen a side.

"We must join their ranks!" shouted Bernardo's brother, and everyone in the room tacitly agreed.

Being a cautious man, Bernardo thought it over for a moment before reaching out for his son's hand. "Come," he said, "I know that no matter what I do, or however severe my warnings, your curiosity will get the best of you. So before you find a way to slip away unnoticed, we shall witness this together."

Within seconds Bernardo filed out the door with his brother, father-in-law, and Niccolò in tow. Bartolommea protested, not for the reason that she thought it unwise for them to rush into harm's way, but because they assumed she would prefer to remain home. She was never one to back off from a good fight. But after a moment's discussion at the front door with Bernardo and her father, she relented, deciding instead that she would do her part by looking after the children and her ailing mother.

Bernardo led Niccolò and his father-in-law into the chaos on via Guicciardini, and merged with the continual flow of bodies rushing toward the center of the city. As they funneled onto the narrow walkway of the Ponte Vecchio, young Niccolò squeezed his father's hand as tightly as he could for fear of being trampled. Once on the other side of the bridge, the marchers met weavers, dyers, peddlers, and day laborers, all part of the *popolo minuto* from the neighboring districts of Santa Croce, Santa Maria Novella, San Lorenzo, and San Marco. They advanced in large clusters, like swarms of locusts, toward their common goal, the Palazzo Vecchio.

When Bernardo and Niccolò entered the piazza, they filtered into the increasingly agitated crowd forming at the base of the palazzo. Their chants of "Medici . . . Medici . . . Medici!" escalated to a fever pitch. What would come of this demonstration of solidarity with the ruling family, and what the people wanted in compensation, was still uncertain, but what held fast was their aversion to the conspiracy and their vote of confidence for the present state of affairs under the Medici. Details of what had actually occurred earlier that morning in the Duomo were shaky, and hard facts as to whether il Magnifico was alive or dead remained elusive. Rumors that he had survived the knife attack were beginning to surface, however, fueling hope among the masses that he could resume control over the city, and emboldening them to shout at the top of their lungs: "Death to the Pazzi!"

As if their wish were a command, two men came flying out of the windows of the upper levels of the Palazzo Vecchio. They were tethered to a rope, a noose fastened securely around their necks. Their bodies came to an abrupt and violent halt when the rope was pulled taut, tightening the noose into a death grip and snapping their necks. The crowd roared its savage approval as the two men dangled above them, kicking and convulsing.

"That is Francesco Pazzi," cried a voice in the crowd, "nephew to Jacopo!"

There was no question of the identity of the other man. Niccolò was certain of it, which prompted his memory to drift back to earlier that day at Holy Mass and his boyish but curiously wise insight on the role the Church played in society. *People are people,* he mused as he watched the body of the Archbishop of Pisa, Francesco Salviati, quiver and slowly lose all signs of life. *People are people.*

Chapter Six

1513: THE DEDICATION

The dandelion salad at the Osteria Casalinga was the finest in the city. Dressed with liberal doses of sea salt, a touch of olive oil, and enough red wine vinegar to cure a head cold, it was the palate cleanser of choice in that part of the peninsula. The owner, Alvaro, always made sure to supply Niccolò with plenty of fresh greens whenever he visited. Being the month of December, it proved to be no easy task.

"Another liter of red," said Biagio as Alvaro dropped off a huge bowl of salad and two plates. He hoped that priming Niccolò with ample volumes of wine would prolong their time together. He needed desperately to talk with someone who understood him, a friend who emotionally and intellectually engaged him, and who ultimately spoke the truth. The thought of an ongoing political discourse with a man of Niccolò's insight excited him, and the premise of the "little book" as described by Niccolò piqued his interest.

Books offering advice to aspiring rulers of state had

certainly been written in the past, and the genre was a well-established tradition, but Biagio knew none could be penned by a man of such no-nonsense judgment, wit, savvy, and hard-boiled experience. Classical authors went to great lengths to suggest that a prince had to display certain virtues in order to effectively hold power and achieve glory: courage, justice, temperance, and prudence. In addition, the qualities of generosity, fairness, and mercy proved indispensable. Knowing what he knew about his friend, however, Biagio suspected Niccolò's counsel to aspiring princes would be profoundly different, and infinitely more controversial.

"I wanted to write something useful," said Niccolò, "and therefore I had no choice but to offer advice based on reality rather than fantasy."

Biagio had to laugh. "The sad reality is that you will be despised for telling the truth."

Niccolò's smile was bittersweet. "Just as a prince should not worry about being considered ruthless, unjust, or cruel if he does what is necessary to liberate his people or establish true peace, I do not worry about being despised."

Whereas Biagio spent most of his waking hours concerned about what people thought of him, Niccolò couldn't have cared less. Biagio had always envied this quality in his dear friend. It gave off an air of strength; it commanded deep respect, and perhaps most importantly, at least from Biagio's point of view, it made him universally likeable, especially to the women they frequented during their after-hours forays. Niccolò had been a bona fide lady's man in his youth, but it was Biagio who truly reaped the benefits by always being faithfully at his side. In fact, Biagio's number one topic of discussion these days was his love life. He'd been waiting for the right moment, without success, throughout this whole lunch to broach the subject of his new paramour with his old friend.

Now that Niccolò had entered middle age, and the pressures of advising the often-clueless Signoria were lifted, his priorities had shifted. Long nights of carousing with friends through back alleys, taverns, and brothels no longer adequately met his needs or released his built-up stress. The fervor he once had for striking deals to benefit the Republic, or for negotiating treaties, was now being channeled into a pragmatic acceptance of solitude and long hours of contemplation in his study. Instead of finding satisfaction in securing the peace as the city's ambassador, which often came at the expense of a neighboring ally, Niccolò had now set his sights on loftier goals such as using the power of the pen to advance unity and lasting peace on the entire peninsula. If anything, his passion for analyzing politics had heightened, and although Biagio couldn't have been prouder to be among the few men in whom Niccolò so generously confided, all Biagio desperately wanted at the moment was to reveal the name of his new love.

Niccolò scooped up a healthy forkful of dandelions. In many respects this was his favorite part of the meal. Like a true Florentine, he appreciated the uncomplicated sobriety of a common salad serving as the meal's final course. A perfect metaphor for life, he thought. He liked how the coarse leaves required careful chewing, providing him ample opportunity to ruminate and ponder his next words.

"What if I dedicated the book to the pope's young nephew?" Niccolò asked.

"Lorenzo de' Medici?" replied Biagio, a bit taken aback. "Would he even read it? He may soon be our ruler, but he hardly bears the intellect of his old namesake."

"One needn't be the Lorenzo il Magnifico of old to grasp the notions I have outlined in this book," said Niccolò. "I haven't filled its pages with high literary phrases and conceits."

Biagio averted his eyes, not eager to spout his next few words: "This may well be true, but there is always the fact that you are not of—"

"No, I am not of noble blood," Niccolò interjected. "You are correct, but I will prevail upon our friend, Vettori, to present it to him."

"I am sorry, Machia, but he is still no Magnifico," replied Biagio. Many of Niccolò's old friends and colleagues often referred to him as "il Machia," an affectionate moniker he acquired in his youth.

"I cannot say whether it is an ominous coincidence or indeed a serendipitous one for our generation to live under the rule of one Lorenzo during our youth, and yet another one as old men," said Niccolò, "but should he read my book, he will learn in a very short time what I have gathered from experience with modern events, and a careful reading of ancient ones."

"Forgive me, but I must take issue with that statement of yours, my friend, and am forced to wholeheartedly disagree," said Biagio.

Niccolò peered into Biagio's eyes.

Recognizing that cold, piercing stare, Biagio straightened up in his seat, smiled back at Niccolò, and quickly added, "You are mistaken when you call us 'old men.'"

This naturally brought a warm smile to Niccolò's lips, which prompted Biagio to seize the moment by transitioning into a discussion of his new woman and love of his life. But just as he got the first few words out of his mouth, Niccolò interrupted.

"We are both old enough to remember the conspiracy

against il Magnifico and his rule. To most people that is ancient history."

"And that qualifies us as old men?" Biagio shot back, half in jest.

"Older men," said Niccolò. "Would you at least grant me that?"

"A bit older, yes," said Biagio, "although my heart never felt younger."

"Young or old, it is a bit of history we can tell firsthand," said Niccolò, clearly wanting to lend more weight to a conversation he saw turning more frivolous than he cared it to be.

"It was a sad day for our dear city," said Biagio, realizing he had to readjust his strategy.

"Sad days," Niccolò was quick to clarify. "The killing carried on for weeks, months, and even years. I saw the limbs of the dead being dragged about the city and fixed on the points of weapons for all of us to witness."

Biagio responded to that familiar look of determination in Niccolò's eyes, that look of needing desperately to get something off his chest, by filling his cup to the brim with more wine. The images of death and severed body parts had suddenly eradicated any potential to change the subject to one of gaiety and women, but Biagio wagered that more wine might help things along. He filled his own cup while he was at it.

"Conspiracies can be devastating when a prince is despised," said Niccolò. "In such a case he would be wise to fear everything and everyone. I cover this in my little book to some degree."

Biagio lifted his cup in a toast. "To your little book," he quipped.

He and Niccolò clinked cups and drank.

"The Pazzi gravely miscalculated the mood of the city,"

73

continued Niccolò. "I also plan to speak at length precisely of this in the third book of my *Discourses,* which I have interrupted to finish *The Prince.*"

"*Discourses?*" asked Biagio, a bit surprised.

"*Discourses on the First Ten Books of Titus Livius,* to be precise," said Niccolò flatly. "I believe I have mentioned it to you. It speaks of republics, whereas *The Prince,* as you know, deals solely with the nature of principalities."

Biagio shrugged. "Forgive me if I cannot keep up with the fruits of your prolific mind," he said jokingly, but he was clearly impressed.

Niccolò accepted the left-handed compliment with an inscrutable grin and continued his political analysis without missing a beat: "The best defense a prince can have against conspiracies is to be loved by the people."

He was alluding to a fact that few citizens of the day would publically dispute: Il Magnifico's policies back then, no matter how aggressive or tyrannical, had caused surprisingly little hatred among the people. On the political front, his skills as a peacekeeper rivaled those of his grandfather, Cosimo. He renewed Florence's alliance with Milan, the centerpiece of Cosimo's foreign policy, and splintered the dangerous partnership between Naples and the pope against Florence. His literary talents also garnered high praise. He had his tutor, Marsilio Ficino, the celebrated scholar, astrologer, and clergyman, to thank for that, as well as the noted Greek philosopher, Argyropoulos, who had emigrated from Constantinople, and Cristoforo Landino, an erudite scholar of Italian classics. And as a patron of the arts, men such as Michelangelo, Andrea del Verocchio, Botticelli, and many other artists owed their start to Lorenzo. Florentine pride in their city ran strong, and Lorenzo deserved much of the credit for it.

"There can be no denying it was the love of his people that saved il Magnifico and his family from disaster during those horrid days of open revolt," said Niccolò.

"It must be said, however, that he delved perhaps a bit too willingly into the personal affairs of the people," rejoined Biagio, hoping to bring the topic of discussion around to a more emotional, if not intimate, level.

"And therein lay the seed of the plot to assassinate him and his brother," Niccolò said. "The law he had issued just a year earlier denying the Pazzi their vast paternal inheritance set the conspiracy in motion. Men would sooner forget the death of their father than the loss of their patrimony."

There appeared to be no way Biagio could seamlessly guide the conversation in the desired direction, so he decided to try a lighter approach.

"So it was all Lorenzo's fault, you say? It is not like you to exonerate the pope from such dealings, my dear Machia."

"Pope Sixtus IV played his part," said Niccolò. "There can be no doubt of that. He was a friend of the Pazzi. His scheme to expand the Church's territorial possessions in Imola and Faenza, land that fell under Medici jurisdiction, drew Lorenzo's stern opposition, and of course prompted Sixtus to remove the Medici as administrators of the papal finances."

"I wonder to whom he entrusted those finances instead?" asked Biagio sarcastically.

Niccolò snickered, then took a sip of wine as he waited for Biagio to answer his own question.

"Hence Lorenzo's motive for passing that vengeful law

aimed at the Pazzi, the pope's brand-new financiers," said Biagio, stating the obvious, but proud of himself for putting two and two together just the same. "And so Jacopo decided to take revenge," he quickly concluded.

"One would think," said Niccolò, "but poor Jacopo does not deserve the blame. In situations such as these, one must look to those who will benefit most. His nephew, Francesco, no doubt hatched the plot. And as all things pertaining to our cursed peninsula, important religious and political figures offered their full support."

Niccolò's mind automatically drifted back to that fateful Easter morning thirty-five years ago when Francesco Pazzi and the Archbishop of Pisa were thrown from the windows of the Palazzo Vecchio as thousands of citizens leveled insults and indignities. That image had kept young Niccolò awake for weeks and months afterward.

"Pope Sixtus IV eagerly endorsed the plot," said Niccolò. "He sought out the military support of the Kingdom of Naples, the Republic of Siena, and the Duchy of Urbino, hoping to rip Florence from the hands of the Medici for good."

"Is that when the great Federico da Montefeltro joined the conspiracy?" asked Biagio, forgetting for a moment that his primary intent was to share the name of his new love with his best friend.

Niccolò nodded. "As did Giovan Battista da Montesecco, the Vatican's infamous *condottiere*."

"Montesecco?" said Biagio quizzically. "I have never heard his name mentioned in relation to these events."

"The original task of slaying il Magnifico fell to him," said Niccolò, "but since the murders were to take place in the Duomo, he withdrew his involvement at the last minute, unwilling to denigrate a sacred place. Two priests from Volterra eagerly picked up the mantle."

"I suppose it is only fitting that priests be the ones to desecrate the house of God," joked Biagio.

"On Easter Sunday, no less," Niccolò added with a grin.

Biagio laughed. "And while celebrating the sacrament of Holy Communion, to boot!"

"So you do know a bit of your history," commented Niccolò, genuinely impressed.

Biagio smiled defensively. "Every red-blooded Florentine knows that."

Niccolò returned the smile, attempting to soften the insult. "Bernardo Bandini was hired to kill Giuliano," he continued. "As the presiding cardinal lifted the holy sacrament into the air, Bandini attacked Giuliano with nineteen sharp blows of his blade."

Niccolò went on to recount in great detail how Giuliano fell to the ground, lifeless, and how, at the same time, Lorenzo managed to elude the advances of his two attackers, suffering only a minor stab wound to the neck. A dear family friend blocked the assassins' path with his own body, and died heroically in Lorenzo's place. In the chaos that followed, Lorenzo sought refuge in the church sacristy. Realizing the plan had misfired, Jacopo Pazzi rode on horseback throughout the city shouting "Freedom!" as his rallying cry, mistakenly believing the Florentine people would rally to his cause.

"I remember that day like it was yesterday, but the people were rendered deaf to Jacopo's call to arms," Niccolò said with a touch of irony in his voice. "The fortune and generosity of the Medici had made them strangers to the concept of freedom."

"And the two priests?" asked Biagio. "I don't remember what became of them."

"An infuriated mob hunted them down," Niccolò replied, "and hung them in the Piazza della Signoria alongside the Archbishop of Pisa and Francesco Pazzi days later. But Lorenzo's revenge was not yet complete. Medici forces eventually captured Jacopo Pazzi in the hills of Romagna. And as you know, he too was hanged."

Niccolò grew dark. It seemed for a moment as if he were tiring of the conversation. But true to form, he plowed on, relating the devastating fate of the entire Pazzi family.

"All its members were eventually killed or exiled," he said, "and their goods sequestered."

"Now that I think of it, it is difficult to find one person in all of Florence who carries the family name," mused Biagio.

"As all successful princes should strive to be, il Magnifico was not a man of half measures," Niccolò replied. "He permanently suppressed the Pazzi name and their coat of arms. All public records, streets, buildings, and families that carried the Pazzi title were renamed in an attempt to erase them from our memory."

"Not from your memory, I can see."

"Bandini was captured a year later in Constantinople and carted back to the Bargello," said Niccolò, gathering steam. "Then, as you would expect, they tied a noose around his neck and hurled him out the window."

Biagio let this sit for a moment. "For all its cruelty, however, his fate lacked the savagery of poor Jacopo's," he said.

Whether Biagio witnessed the horrors of those days or not, events that left bodies in the streets and hacked limbs on the points of lances were discussed in every Florentine household, tavern, and street corner for years. There was one ferocious and utterly shameful event, however, that topped all the others, and Biagio was surprised Niccolò had stopped short of mentioning it.

But once again, Niccolò did not disappoint. He lowered his eyes in what seemed to be true grief.

"It wasn't so much the sight of bodies thrown from the upper levels of the Palazzo Vecchio that gave me nightmares as a child," Niccolò said, "but the ignominious spectacle of parading the corpse of a once-honorable man up and down the streets of the city."

"You witnessed it?" said Biagio, almost too afraid to ask.

"Just days after Jacopo was buried, a mob of Medici zealots exhumed his body, mutilated it, and reburied it, only to dig it up again and drag it through the city by the very noose that was used to hang him, said Niccolò. "Via Guicciardini appeared to be one of their favorite thoroughfares. They eventually threw Jacopo's body into the Arno."

"Would Saint Peter, or Satan himself, accept someone into their realm after such desecration?" said Biagio mortified.

"Even the wealthy and the most powerful can lose everything through imprudence, reckless ambition, and the whims of fortune," mused Niccolò. And with that, he knocked down the rest of his wine.

Biagio sat silent a while. When Alvaro arrived to gather up their plates, Biagio threw a couple of florins on the table in payment. Niccolò nodded his thanks and playfully slapped his friend on the back to show his appreciation. It went without saying that Biagio would pick up the tab, partly out of respect for his former boss, and partly as a tacit acknowledgment of Niccolo's dire financial state, but mostly to make it easier to share his sentiments about the new woman in his life, which Biagio knew would be a difficult pill for Niccolò to swallow. She was, after all, someone that Niccolò knew very well, and definitely not a person about whom he would, or could, remain neutral.

As they got up to leave, Biagio stopped and stared into his old friend's eyes. Niccolò stared back. He could tell Biagio had something to reveal, so Niccolò just stood there waiting for him to spit it out.

"I'm in love," Biagio finally whispered, hardly able to wipe the grin of happiness mixed with pure dread from his face.

Niccolò didn't move or utter a word; the slight turn of a smile registered as his only reaction. He knew from history that Biagio's tastes ran parallel to his own, often centering around the same type of woman: a widow, or unhappy wife, but more often than not a local courtesan with a sharp tongue and an even sharper brain in her head. The posture of the two men, their unwavering glares, and their protracted silence took on all the airs of a standoff, both hoping to God that no emotional territory had been, or would be, breached, and that their manly honor, however tender and volatile, would remain intact. Niccolò caught a glimpse of joy beginning to surge in Biagio's expression, which managed to thaw the impasse.

"In love?" Niccolò quipped. "Again?" This evoked a genuine chuckle from Biagio, and Niccolò's body language softened. "I'm happy for you," he continued. "Anyone I know?"

Biagio's anxiety hinged precisely on the fact that Niccolò knew her all too well. In fact, he had spent a good amount of time in her company. Niccolò often visited her after particularly stressful trips abroad during his time as ambassador. Marietta, his wife, tolerated his late-night escapades to a certain degree. Niccolò was a loving husband, a doting father, and a steady provider, but whether he was faithful to their bond of marriage remained a topic Marietta preferred to leave unattended. She never even posed the question, perhaps knowing too well what the answer would be. Her turn of a blind eye to his philandering put a strain on their relationship at times, but for the most part she endured it. In effect, Niccolò's itch to roam didn't bother Marietta as much as her husband's long trips abroad while at the Second Chancery. She feared for his welfare and worried about the dangers he faced in those foreign lands. Marietta's rock-solid character and uncanny skill to compartmentalize her duties as a wife and mother, as well as her ability to keep her expectations at a realistic level, ensured her sanity, and it was precisely this sanity and levelheadedness that Niccolò loved about her. Ultimately, however, as with most women throughout Niccolò's life, she had him wrapped around her little finger, which is ironically how he liked it.

The answer to "Anyone I know?" was a long time coming. Niccolò had perceived his friend's trepidation early on in their conversation, but thought it better not to address it. So he just waited until Biagio found the courage to speak up.

"Lucrezia," he finally spurted.

"Lucrezia?" said Niccolò. "Which Lucrezia do you mean exactly . . . my Lucrezia?"

Biagio could only manage a shrug. "Well, I don't know if you can actually call her 'your Lucrezia,' now that—"

"La Riccia?" interjected Niccolò.

Biagio nodded sheepishly. "Now that you no longer live in the city, I don't believe she—"

"The Lucrezia known as La Riccia?" asked Niccolò. "*My* La Riccia?" The two men locked eyes, stone-faced. "You've been visiting her?"

Biagio decided to wait for the semblance of a smile, or some other signal of acceptance, to make its way onto Niccolò's face before venturing a response.

Niccolò, for his part, was doing everything he could to prolong his friend's agony by suppressing the laugh he'd been dying to let loose since Biagio's little confession began. This type of scene had branded the two men for as long as they'd known each other, a rivalry going all the way back to the early days of their friendship, a time in both their lives filled with intense study at the university by day and wild adventures into Florence's shadowy red-light district by night. It was also a period that coincided with harsh political and social turmoil for the city of Florence and the entire Italian peninsula. In the end, it was the very remembrance of those turbulent days that finally prompted a silly grin to appear on Niccolò's face.

"Have I visited her?" Biagio repeated, buying time. "Actually, quite often," he finally admitted.

He braced himself for Niccolò's grin to turn itself upside down. The opposite happened. Niccolò burst out laughing.

"Why don't we go there now?" said Niccolò, leading the way.

A visibly relieved Biagio gladly followed.

Chapter Seven

The years immediately following the upheaval brought on by the Pazzi conspiracy passed in relative peace and prosperity for the city of Florence. Lorenzo il Magnifico subsequently gained even more power and influence after a successful round of diplomacy to avert war with Pope Sixtus IV and the Kingdom of Naples. And with peace came an era of corruption, and years of moral weakness and civil degradation.

By 1494, at the age of twenty-five, young Niccolò had grown to become a dedicated student at the University of Florence. His maturity far surpassed that of his boyhood friends and schoolmates, and his wisdom and perspicacity rivaled, and often eclipsed, that of most of his learned professors. He could already observe, for example, as if he were a man twice his age with twice the experience, that the inordinate level of frivolity and immoderation present among his peers spelled disaster for his city's future. "These are evils generated by people who have grown accustomed to the seductive comforts of peace," he often declaimed to fellow students during their frequent, and often quite rowdy, political debates.

"We spend beyond our means on food, dress, gambling, women, and all sorts of leisurely pleasures," said Niccolò during one of these very debates in Piazza San Marco, not far from the halls of the university.

Also intermingled among this group of aspiring lawyers and civil servants, but who remained conspicuously outside the inner circle, stood the twenty-one-year-old Biagio Buonaccorsi. He began his studies a few years after Niccolò, so they hadn't yet met on a formal basis. Both were attracted to these ad hoc political forums that gathered after the main lectures in the university's grand hall, but Biagio hesitated to participate fully due to his first-year status. Ever since his very first meeting, however, he noticed that Niccolò's knowledge of history, both ancient and contemporary, and his keen powers of persuasion made him a force to be reckoned with. Others in the group also sensed Niccolò's superior grasp of world events and their influences, positive and negative, on their beloved Florence, but that hardly kept them from throwing themselves into the discussions. Far from it.

"I couldn't agree more!" shouted a young student. "We have drifted too far from God's grace and must mend our ways."

"Pious remedies have no place in our city," Niccolò shot back.

"Do you doubt the inspired words of the friar?" replied the young student. He was referring to a Dominican friar from Ferrara, Girolamo Savonarola, who had been condemning the rapacity of the wealthy class, denouncing Florence's moral decay, and proclaiming the coming of the Apocalypse with frightening regularity since his rise to prominence in the city in 1491.

The constant drumbeat of his admonishments and dire warnings produced a debilitating effect on the hearts and minds of everyday Florentines. After the death of il Magnifico in April of 1492 and the ignominious fall from power of his son, Piero, the following year, the city fathers, with plenty of backing from the French, finally ousted the Medici from power. Savonarola became Florence's political and spiritual leader, and plans for a new, free republic eventually saw the light of day.

"Do I doubt the friar's words?" repeated Niccolò with gusto. "I hail his ability to foresee Italy's pains, and I share his negative assessment of poor Piero as a leader whose dishonorable behavior generated even more corruption in the people." His voice grew firmer: "A prince must always maintain the appearance of integrity."

In essence, however, Niccolò's opinions of Savonarola were mixed. He considered the friar to be a keen observer, and a prophet of sorts, but wasn't as taken with his moralistic solutions for solving Florence's many problems. Florentines, in Niccolò's eyes, harbored a much more complex and contradictory spirit. On one hand, they sang licentious songs in the streets with abandon during Carnival, and on the other, they would chant the church's most sacred hymns using those identical rhyme schemes and rhythms, on those same city streets. Niccolò himself embodied a similar contradictory outlook on life. Behind his stern exterior hid a smirk just waiting to emerge. He fused *gravitas* with playful mischief, cold objectivity with passion, and dark political realism with an idealistic desire to untether Italy from foreign dependence and domination.

"And I would assume you also do not question Savonarola's disdain for the corruption within the Church of Rome," said the young student.

"As to that, the friar speaks the truth and must be lauded," replied Niccolò. "But his insistence on prayer, abstinence from food and sex, and most forms of entertainment as a panacea for all our ills will hardly guarantee our freedom, or political stability. He strays too far from humanity's natural instincts."

"The good friar's persuasive talents serve us well in keeping the peace with our neighbors," another in the group cried out.

"Yet he incessantly predicts pestilence, famine, and the ruination of Florence from the pulpit," said Niccolò. "This is not peace! And this will not save us from the French or any other invader."

The group went silent. No one could refute him. As much as Savonarola's promise of stability and a return to true Christian values enticed the populous, his prophecies of disaster on the horizon chilled them to the bone. His opposition to the intellectual curiosity that Florence had fostered since the time of Dante, Petrarch, and Boccaccio ran contrary to the Florentine spirit; it negated more than a century of scholarly investigation of the classics and cast aspersions on the notion of human dignity championed by such luminaries as Bracciolini, Bruni, and della Mirandola.

Truth be told, Niccolò had little tolerance for friars in general, and made no bones about it. He held them to be self-indulgent, avaricious, and even lustful frauds. However, despite Niccolò's complete lack of confidence in Savonarola's ability to negotiate wider peace for his native city or to secure protection from an imminent French invasion, he intuitively understood the futility and inherent danger of openly criticizing him.

"I have spoken my mind," he went on to declare to the group, "but it must also be said that one ought not speak with irreverence of so prodigious a man."

At this point, Biagio couldn't keep his mouth shut any

longer. "The fact remains that since Lorenzo's death there has been no one on the entire peninsula with the prudence to check the ambitions and political wrangling of the Republic of Venice, the Kingdom of Naples, the Vatican, and in particular Milan, who sees war as its best opportunity to gain power."

"What brings this apologist for the Medici into our midst?" shouted the young student.

"We must all celebrate the fact that the tyranny of the Medici has vanished from our city," said Biagio. "For the first time in our lives, the dream of a true republic can be made real. But make no mistake, a careful observation of past events tells us that il Magnifico expertly managed to broker a tender balance of power between our unpredictable neighbors."

Niccolò listened to Biagio's retort with great satisfaction. *Finally, someone besides me who can put these idiots in their place,* he thought to himself. He offered Biagio a friendly nod.

For his part, Biagio acknowledged Niccolò with a quick smile, and continued with his outpouring, but this time directly at Niccolò: "It is noble to say that Savonarola must be treated with reverence, but we cannot remain silent when war is at hand, and—"

"Savonarola will protect us," interjected one of the students.

Niccolò jumped in. "Let our young colleague speak," he said, indicating Biagio.

Biagio was, of course, correct. The European political landscape had grown increasingly precarious over the last few years, a harsh reality that greatly worried Niccolò, who kept abreast of events on the world stage with fiery diligence. Rumors of war were ringing out loud and clear from all corners of the continent. Charles VIII, the king of France, had been threatening an invasion of the Kingdom of Naples for years, thanks to an old Angevin claim to the kingdom. But now that Charles stood at Italy's doorstep with plans to sweep southward through the territories of Milan, Florence, and the Papal State to conquer the Kingdom of Naples, the horrors of war loomed larger than ever. Meanwhile, the major Italian city-states, rather than band together and rally against the French king to safeguard their integrity, demonstrated either a lack of will, firepower, or simple courage to discourage him. To add insult to injury, the death of il Magnifico coincided with the rise of two notorious leaders on the Italian peninsula: Rodrigo Borgia to the south, who became Pope Alexander VI, and Ludovico Sforza to the north, the impetuous duke of Milan. Both were shrewd statesmen bent on land expansion, and both more than willing to use France's deadly artillery as leverage to achieve their ends.

With his finger still indicating Biagio, Niccolò continued, "The man clearly sees, as do I, that Savonarola offers little by way of any armed resistance to credibly contain the French advance onto our peninsula."

"It is not the French who will bring destruction," cried out the student in rebuttal, "but our unholy actions against God. These are not my words, but the prophecies of Frá Savonarola."

Others chimed in with similar expressions of support for the friar.

"War on the peninsula is imminent, and its dominion by foreign powers inevitable," added Niccolò firmly. "You may call it God's retribution if it suits you, but in the end it will be our inaction in the face of conflict that condemns us to a lifetime of foreign subjugation."

"Charles VIII must first pass through the Duchy of Milan!" shouted one in the group.

"Ludovico Sforza cannot be trusted," answered Biagio, who by now had inserted himself fully into the circle.

"He would go so far as to instigate an invasion hoping to take advantage of the chaos that would certainly follow," said Niccolò, "and the Borgia pope is no better. His hatred for the King of Naples will only further exacerbate the intrigue between all the states that surround us."

"And the friar's explosive rhetoric only makes matters worse," said Biagio.

The young student stiffened with anger. "You sound worse than the Arrabbiati who poison the minds of our citizens."

"And you are nothing more than one of his obedient Piagnoni!" shouted Biagio.

The young student did not recoil at the charge. In fact, he may have reveled in it. The Piagnoni, or "Wailers," clung to the principles and beliefs of Savonarola with unabashed fervor. They acquired the name because of their cries of exhilaration and despair during his sermons. Those who opposed the friar were dubbed Arrabbiati, or "Angry Ones," due to their indignation over the increasing austerity imposed upon the population. Savonarola condemned all avenues of entertainment and displays of luxury, public or private. Gambling, card playing, backgammon, and other games of chance faced the friar's particular wrath, as did prostitution, a favorite pastime and form of amusement for many Florentine men.

"My anger has less to do with the personal restriction placed upon me, although I must confess I loathe them with a passion," said Niccolò, "and more to do with the need for prudent governance."

"And who is to decide what constitutes luxury and

entertainment?" shouted Biagio, now the only one actively in agreement with Niccolò.

"It is the friar who decides," countered yet another student joining the circle.

"The friar's demise will come precisely because of his suppression of the very freedoms to which we have all become accustomed," Niccolò cried.

The young student interjected, "He has been chosen by God to lead us away from the corruption of Rome and toward our redemption . . ."

The resounding cry of hundreds of voices in the distance muffled the young student's last few words. A flock of shabbily dressed boys, all barely twelve years old, rounded the corner by the church of San Marco chanting "Redemption!" at the top of their lungs. Indignation and righteousness twisted their innocent faces into masks of fiendish rage. The group of debaters in the piazza, including Niccolò and Biagio, dropped everything to watch the impassioned caravan of boys, each clutching an object firmly to his chest. One held an amateur painting of Venus, another an elaborately gilded looking glass, and a third an armful of books and scrolls. They were followed by dozens of other youths carrying strings of pearls, wigs, wall mirrors, chessboards, reams of books, and scores of paintings and other works of art.

Their chanting grew increasingly shrill as they marched down the narrow street leading to the Duomo. Savonarola had recruited, brainwashed, and empowered these fanatical youths to hustle door-to-door throughout the city in order to sequester "vanity" items from the homes of unsuspecting Florentines, preying on their guilt and shame. Like so many events of importance or circumstance in Florence, the final destination was always the Piazza della Signoria. Once there, the boys would ceremoniously toss their items, one by one, atop a massive pile of kindling wood primed to ignite a ritualistic "bonfire of the vanities." The event attracted thousands of eager Piagnoni, who stood obsequiously at the foot of the raging pyre singing hymns to the Lord and chanting their praises to Savonarola. Thousands of onlookers inevitably found their way into the piazza as well, many of whom were respected government officials seeking to ingratiate themselves with the friar. Men of influence too proud to mingle with the frenzied devotees made up a good part of the multitude as well, but most were just ordinary Florentines hungry for a night of entertainment.

Niccolò and Biagio certainly fell into this last category of onlookers. They followed the chanting boys from San Marco past the Piazza del Duomo and the Baptistery, down the via dei Calzaiuoli, and into the Piazza della Signoria, where they secured a spot on the upper steps of the Palazzo Vecchio with a clear view of the unholy sacrament about to take place at the far end of the square. They watched and listened, somewhat uncomfortably, as the Piagnoni's cries of jubilation gradually transformed into a single harmonic chord heard throughout the city, slowly intensifying in pitch and volume. Plumes of smoke twisted through the huge stack of pulpwood and heaved skyward. When flames burst through the smoke, the unified cry of the Piagnoni cleaved into hundreds of separate expressions of pure rapture.

The entire piazza stood mesmerized as the crackle of burning timber and the retching of flames became an all-encompassing spectacle of sight and sound. Individual citizens, intoxicated by what they perceived to be a glorious purification ritual, plodded forward, painstakingly weaving their way through the masses, each wielding vanity items gleaned from their own homes to be consumed in the bonfire, where the promise of lasting redemption awaited them. One by one, they tossed their objects into the fire as the crowd roared its approval: hand mirrors, combs, brooches, shoes, wedding rings, bracelets, cosmetics, ornaments of all shapes and sizes, heraldic totems of every variety, badges, coats of arms, insignias, all genres of literature, history books, epic poems, love letters, artistic drawings, carvings, paintings, engravings, and even wooden trinkets found their way into the growing firestorm.

Niccolò marveled at the theatrics of it all, simultaneously appalled by the depths to which his beloved city had fallen and fascinated by the ease with which the sermons of a simple Dominican friar could manipulate common citizens and divert them from their everyday beliefs and customs.

"I find it disheartening to know that Charles of France can penetrate the Alps," said Niccolò to Biagio, "with an alleged force of twelve thousand infantrymen, thousands of Swiss troops, Gascons, and cavalrymen, and enough artillery guns to level an entire city, or so they say, while we Florentines are reduced to this sad farce."

Biagio pointed to a handsome blond gentleman wending his way through the horde, clutching an elegantly framed portrait of a young woman. She had blonde hair as well; her lips were curled into a mischievous smile and her eyes glimmered a translucent blue. Biagio's jaw dropped at the sight of her, and Niccolò, too, fell captive to her gaze. A more beautiful woman had never been created by the hand of a mere mortal.

"The man is a magician," said Biagio as the gentleman continued to filter into the mob, inching closer to the fire.

"He is Botticelli," said Niccolò, "an artist of some repute."

Niccolò had actually met Botticelli a few years earlier with his father in the company of Bartolomeo Scala, the old gonfalonier. Alessandro di Mariano di Vanni Filipepi, known as Sandro Botticelli, painted hundreds of religious pieces in a style reminiscent of many of the older painters that graced the Medici stable of artists throughout the 1460s and '70s: Fra Filippo Lippi, the Pollaiuolo brothers, and one of the greatest masters of the era, Andrea del Verrocchio. However, il Magnifico preferred Botticelli's more classically inspired paintings, where his prepossessing Roman deities and pagan goddesses celebrated the ideal of heavenly beauty in a decidedly temporal form. The woman in the painting was just such a goddess, and anathema to the morals of the Dominican friar.

"I cannot allow him to destroy a thing of such magnificence," said Biagio. "I must stop him."

Niccolò grabbed Biagio by the arm to halt his advance. "I have only just met you, but I don't believe you would be such a fool."

"You have no idea the levels of idiocy I would achieve for the sake of a beautiful woman."

"I see we not only share the same view of politics and the world," said Niccolò with a wicked smile, "but of women as well."

The smile on Niccolò's face turned immediately sour as Botticelli penetrated the empty space at the fire's edge that was suddenly created by the multitude of Piagnoni retreating from the infernal heat. Botticelli wiped the beads of sweat from his brow; he gripped the portrait firmly in both hands and raised it above his head as a gesture to God, pleading for His mercy, and acknowledging his sin of pride for his art. He bowed in reverence as if standing before a sacred altar.

"Forgive me, oh Lord!" he screamed.

Then all at once, his eyes widened like a man possessed. His features darkened. Peace and serenity abandoned him. Nothing holy or sacred remained. All the latent resentment of having to sacrifice his art, his life's work, rose unexpectedly to the surface. His conversion to the pious Christianity promulgated by the friar suddenly betrayed a chink in its armor. A flicker of his former humanity burst through to reveal the creativity, love of logic, harmony, and beauty he once knew. For a moment, he stood ready to denounce his newborn faith in Savonarola's wrathful God. But that glorious flash of reason lasted but a split second, overtaken by the memory of the friar's hypnotic words: "May the sword of God smite this earth and return me to thee!"

Botticelli screamed it aloud. "May the sword of God smite this earth and return me to thee!"

The scowl of righteousness worn by all of Savonarola's faithful returned to him. Redemption was at hand. Botticelli could feel it. All he had to do was release the portrait from the fury of his grip, let it merge with all of Florence's vainglorious debris, and watch it burn until it was no more. Only in this way could his sins be forgiven and could the city of his birth escape the ire of a vengeful God. He knew this to be true. *There could be no greater form of patriotism,* he thought to himself.

The moment the portrait left the artist's hands, Niccolò realized he had seen enough. "Let us leave this wretched place," he called out to Biagio, who stood horrified as the image of the most beautiful woman in the world dissolved before his eyes, consumed in the fire within seconds.

Having completed his selfless act, Botticelli fell to his knees in prayer. Tears welled up in his eyes, his body went limp, and he collapsed onto the cobblestone.

By now, Niccolò and Biagio had made their way through

the frenzied crowd, eager to get as far away from Piazza della Signoria as possible.

"I know of a friendly little place in the San Frediano," said Biagio, doing all he could to turn the horror of what he had just witnessed into something more pleasurable. "The women there don't care a fig about Savonarola or his condemnation of them."

Niccolò was in the prime of his life. He was an intelligent, resourceful, intuitive, perceptive, judicious, and reasonably handsome young university student. His future at twenty-five years of age looked bright, and he could find no logical reason to reject Biagio's offer. *To do anything else would be unnatural,* he thought to himself.

They fought against the tide of bodies streaming toward the unholy bonfire and crossed the grassy knoll leading to the Arno. It was their best path to sanity. When they finally reached the river, they made a beeline for that friendly little place in the San Frediano.

Chapter Eight

1513: OLD FRIENDS AND COURTESANS

To look at La Riccia you would think she was of noble birth. She donned the clothing of the wealthy class, perhaps bought for her in her youth by a rich count or lovesick merchant, which allowed her to mix freely in the churches, piazzas, and marketplaces with the so-called "respectable" women of the city. The differences in appearance between her, a noted courtesan, and a reputable marquess or the wife of an influential banker were minimal: La Riccia routinely wore a square décolletage just a fraction lower, and more revealing, than usual; a slightly tighter bodice; an intricately embroidered gown, usually red, with brocades of silk, and braids, couching, trimming, beading, and pearls a shade more overstated than the norm. She rarely left the house deprived of her feathered cap, platform shoes, cabochon rings, pearl necklace, and silk fan to protect herself from the heat and nagging humidity of the Florentine summer. And high mass on Sundays required that she add a black translucent veil, as well as jeweled rosary beads suspended ostentatiously from her girdle, to her repertoire.

To see a large number of such well-dressed women in the churches of Florence, so striking in appearance and pious in demeanor, was hardly unusual. If you paid close attention, you might see a few well-placed curls falling provocatively out of their caul or netted cap as they kept their eyes modestly lowered and their hands joined in solemn prayer; no doubt you would also notice a shawl placed ever so strategically over their shoulders to expose their ivory white skin, and just enough of their ample bosom to claim respectability. When the Holy Mass ended, and the congregation uniformly exited the church in haste, they usually lingered a bit longer than expected in the piazza, or on the steps of the church itself, to field the advances of certain men, often figures of high influence and impeccable reputation.

It was on just such a Sunday morning, three years ago, at the ripe age of forty-one and at the height of his fame as Florence's foreign ambassador, that Niccolò made La Riccia's acquaintance. He had seen her numerous times plying her trade in broad daylight, under the very nose of the Church, but for one reason or another he never approached her. He couldn't resist for long, however. The stress of his many years in the Second Chancery had evidently taken its toll. From that fateful morning forward, he paid frequent visits to her residence around the corner from the church of Ognissanti. Sometimes he would come with Biagio to talk, play cards, and simply enjoy the company of a charming, bright, and hospitable younger woman. Biagio's affinity for so-called "emancipated" women became evident to Niccolò ever since their visit to the San Frediano after the "bonfire of the vanities" nearly twenty years ago. The events of that night formed a particular bond between the two men that endured until this day. However, as might be expected, Niccolò would often visit La Riccia alone when in need of more intimacy. Being well educated and quite versed in the classics, La Riccia used these moments to recite the sonnets of Petrarch or sing a gentle aria as a prelude to their evening's activities.

For his part, Biagio always remained mindful of Niccolò's special bond with "dear dear La Riccia," as he called her. He looked but he did not touch. Niccolò obviously could not claim exclusivity over her. By definition of her occupation she frequented other men—several other men, in fact—but Biagio managed to keep his distance just the same, out of respect for his friend, and despite La Riccia's overly flirtatious mien when in his presence, which tested every ounce of his self-control, to say the least. All that changed, however, after the Republic fell back into Medici hands last year, after he and Niccolò had lost their long-held positions in the government, and especially after Niccolò's exile from Florence to his country farm in the Albergaccio.

No meal at the Casalinga would be complete without paying a visit to their favorite courtesan, especially after Biagio professed his love for her without either a harsh word or rebuff from his dear friend. During their stroll along the Lungarno, the path paralleling the river, and past the church of Santa Maria del Carmine, over the Ponte alla Carraia, and down the Borgo Ognissanti to La Riccia's house, the two men worked out their petty grievances. They decided that quibbling over the love of a woman benefitted no one. Given Niccolò's sense of reason and overall acceptance of La Riccia's powerful lure, he resigned himself to the fact that he owned no part of her, or ever could. After all, Biagio's sentiments had to be acknowledged and respected. They agreed, and Niccolò insisted, that their friendship transcend such petty squabbles, and that Niccolò's desire to have Biagio critique *The Prince* took preference over everything else. Niccolò had no doubts as to his priorities: His treatise would make its way to Lorenzo de' Medici's desk, and he would read it. All else would have to wait, including an evening with the most charming and entertaining courtesan in all of Florence. They had work to do. They agreed that they would simply pay her their respects and be on their way, or so they hoped.

Her arrival at the door clad in a lace chemise had them alter their plans somewhat. After all, what could be the harm in spending a few choice hours in good company?

La Riccia smiled at the two men, who stood at the foot of the steps like lovesick schoolboys, and ushered them in with genuine enthusiasm, which only made their decision to leave early and head for Sant'Andrea before sunset more difficult. And, of course, seating them on a finely upholstered sofa in the intimacy of her bedroom while serving them fresh baked *biscotti di Prato* and a bottle of rare Madeira wine weakened their resolve beyond repair. La Riccia infected everyone she knew with her unadulterated joy for life, making her irresistible to men and women alike.

But Niccolò knew the other side of her as well. He had fallen victim to her penchant for speaking her mind—especially regarding the pomposity of men—on more than one occasion, which, it could be argued, had the positive effect of keeping him on the straight and narrow. "You may be the high lord of diplomats, and the prince of politics with kings and popes, but you know nothing of women," she repeatedly told him in one form or another. Even when she attempted to ease the brunt of her harsh criticism by qualifying her attack to include all men, her words stung like the deadly pinch of a scorpion. "Men . . .

I don't know what goes on in their tiny heads," she would say. "All they know how to do is turn everything upside down." Deep inside, knowing what Niccolò knew about the sad state of affairs on the continent, a world run entirely by men, he could not in good conscience disagree with her.

"Well, Christmas has come early for me," she whispered with a genuine smile as she rested three glasses of fine crystal on a refectory table. The rich Madeira wine poured like warm honey. She filled each vessel to the brim.

"May we share many more such Christmases," said Biagio, raising his glass in tribute.

"Here, here," rejoined Niccolò, suddenly at a loss for anything of substance to say.

La Riccia often had this enervating effect on him. *She's smarter than any crafty head of state,* he often thought to himself, and a lot more persuasive than any silver-tongued diplomat with whom he'd ever had to negotiate a truce. At times he just stood in awe of the raw, natural power she wielded: the power to advance notions of civility, harmony, and humanity's basic longing for peace. Niccolò's genius for seeing the truth behind the obscurity of most things revealed time and time again, in no uncertain terms, that the morals put forward by the Church, or the laws established by an all-powerful sovereign state, had much to learn from a woman like her. She somehow made her stable of men forget their petty jealousies and rivalries, inducing them instead to appreciate the worldly pleasures she offered. Her approach to life refuted the standard logic of war where one side must destroy the other; rather, it fostered an environment in which both parties could strive, unhindered, to achieve their goals, and both could ultimately claim victory.

Finally, after an awkward silence with Niccolò fumbling for the right words to add to his prosaic toast, the three of them simply clinked their glasses together and drank.

"The countryside has been good to you, my dear Niccolò," she said, breaking the silence. "It has added brawn to that delicate body of yours."

"I thank you, Riccia my dear, you are kind as always," said Niccolò, "but of late I have lifted nothing but a meager quill from my desk, and have exercised only my uncallused fingers to scrawl a few words here and there."

"Don't be fooled by the man's false modesty, Riccia my dear," said Biagio, doing nothing to hide his pride in his friend. "Our illustrious Machia has transformed himself into an author who will one day join the ranks of Xenophon, Livy, and Pliny the Elder."

"I see I share the company of two kind friends today," Niccolò responded.

"I forgot to add, of course, that you have absolutely no chance of joining those ranks without the help of dear Biagio Buonaccorsi here," said Biagio, betraying a smirk. "How can someone like you, who has read all there is to read and experienced everything a poor diplomat could possibly experience, succeed all alone? And do not forget, I was with you on that horrid morning of the French king's entrance into our fair city."

Niccolò summoned the memories of that fateful event. "What you say is true, my friend. It was also the very day I decided my destiny would be as a civil servant." He then turned his attention to La Riccia: "Dear Biagio and I have shared everything ever since our first meeting nearly twenty years ago." He was, of course, alluding to their visit to the bordello in the San Frediano.

A sly grin formed on La Riccia's lips. "And I surmise you would like to continue to share everything now that you find yourselves in the Borgo Ognissanti!" she said with a sultry wink.

Before they could answer, she poured them another glass of Madeira.

Chapter Nine

1494: STICKS OF CHALK

Just a few weeks after the unholy bonfire in the Piazza della Signoria, the French army had descended deep into the Italian peninsula and taken hold of the Romagna region northeast of Florence. On his way southward, King Charles VIII stopped outside the gates of Mordano requesting immediate entrance into the city. When his demands were refused, the king's cannons blasted through its robust ramparts, completely destroying the city and decimating its population. The same fate befell the town of Fivizzano in Lunigiana just six days later. Ambassadors of all the Italian states traveled furiously around the peninsula warning of the "devilish machinery" at the king's disposal, asserting without hesitation that his artillery was capable of demolishing any existing fortification on the continent. Imagine the terror in the hearts of Florence's citizenry when word spread that the French had settled on the outskirts their city.

The young Niccolò had been kept abreast of Charles's progress by Marcello Virgilio Adriani, his professor at the university, with whom he had formed a tight teacher-student relationship. It didn't take long for Adriani to realize that Niccolò's talents as a political analyst rose above all the rest. A *bona fide* humanist who knew Greek and Latin to perfection as well as medicine and the natural sciences, Adriani studied under Cristoforo Landino and the recently deceased poet and classical scholar Angelo Poliziano. Considered by all to be a judicious man of noble demeanor with a gift for eloquence, he also enjoyed close ties with key officials deep within the nascent free Republic under Friar Savonarola's leadership, which in turn made him privy to sensitive matters evolving behind the scenes. Of particular concern to Niccolò—and indeed to all Florentines, not the least of which was Savonarola himself— were Charles's intentions now that he'd crossed the Alps and descended, unencumbered, into the heartland of Italy.

Niccolò learned from Adriani that the seeds of war were sown many years earlier by Ludovico Sforza, known as "il Moro," when he successfully conspired to take possession of the city of Milan to become its de facto lord. Without any legal rights to the position, Ludovico found himself surrounded by enemies and plagued by the constant fear of attack. He narrowly survived a conspiracy in 1485, and just four years later the rightful successor to the throne in Milan, Giovan Galeazzo Visconti, married Isabella of Aragon, the niece to King Ferrante of Naples, posing a tangible threat to Ludovico's legitimacy. Rather than relinquish his ill-gotten power, Ludovico secretly encouraged Charles VIII to hasten his proposed invasion of Italy and take possession of the Kingdom of Naples. Ludovico speculated that amid all the chaos of war he could carve out more land and influence for himself to the south of Milan's territories. His prodding of Charles played right into the French king's grandiose plans of using Italy as a jumping-off point to fight the Turks.

With the threat of war at Italy's doorstep, diplomacy became a booming occupation. All the smaller states in the northern part of the peninsula scrambled to avoid a conflict with the superior power of the French. Marcello Adriani knew it was simply a matter of time before Florence would have to deal with Charles face-to-face. His conviction that his beloved city needed a talented diplomatic corps to survive the current military escalation of its neighbors remained as strong as ever. He obviously saw great potential in Niccolò. While the ambassadors of Venice stood out for their good sense and political wisdom, Florence excelled in elegance, style, and uncanny precision in analyzing human interaction. The young Niccolò clearly excelled in all those categories.

Nearly a fortnight after a delegation of ambassadors led by Savonarola traveled to the outskirts of the city to meet with the French king in an effort to prevent his armies from ransacking the city, and wreaking havoc on its people, Adriani invited Niccolò to join him for a drink at a tavern in the university district. By now fear had spread throughout the city like the plague, and Adriani was curious to learn what this bright young observer of social and political behavior thought of the whole matter.

Severe *tramontana* winds from the north, and Florence's position deep in the Arno valley, made for cold, damp autumns and frosty winters. Although it was still only November, the icy air of the university's grand hall where Adriani had just completed a two-and-a-half-hour lecture managed to send its students racing home for a steaming bowl of *zuppa di verdura,* or to the local tavern to defrost with colleagues over an aged wine or mulled fruit juice. As soon as Adriani and Niccolò took a seat at a table across from the tavern's massive fireplace, Adriani ordered two warm pomegranate juices—a trendy delicacy of crushed pomegranate kernels spiced with honey, clove, mint, lemon peel, mace, and cinnamon, then heated until its rich scarlet liquid thickened to a drab umber.

"Well, Signor Machiavelli," said Adriani, "what would you say if I told you the friar has offered the French a literal king's ransom to spare our city?"

"Then, my kind Maestro, we should immediately declare victory over a weak and undetermined foe," said Niccolò, obviously unconvinced. "But I fear that the king has not ventured all this way just to squeeze a handful of florins from every Italian prince. He seeks free passage through our territories to facilitate his scheme to overtake the Kingdom of Naples, and nothing less."

Adriani eked out a knowing smile. "I would have been disappointed had you answered in any other manner."

"Allow me to add," said Niccolò, "since our illustrious neighbors have not joined with us to forge a defense against this common aggressor, I would wager our emissaries had to acquiesce much more than a mere king's ransom."

Adriani averted his eyes. Niccolò studied him carefully. His mentor obviously had bad news to report.

"The king demands that we allow him to parade into our fair city, after which we shall host him, and a good number of his officers and troops, for as long as they care to stay," Adriani said timidly. He could barely look his young student in the eyes.

"The friar surely cannot concede to this humiliation," Niccolò stated firmly.

Adriani finally met Niccolò's gaze. "What choice do we have?"

"Our submission must have its limits," said Niccolò. "Nothing will stop this French invader from demanding that we reinstate Medici rule so that he might enjoy the benefits of their power and fealty."

"I trust this would exhaust the patience of every Florentine if we ever reach such a point in our negotiations," said Adriani. "But once again, what do you propose we do against such military superiority?"

As Niccolò was wont to do when posed such questions of import, his eyes locked firmly with those of the man across from him; he remained silent, and offered no facial gestures or the slightest hand movement that would betray his thoughts. Not even the arrival of the craggy old waiter with two steaming mugs of pomegranate juice broke his concentration. Without missing a beat, Niccolò wrapped his gentlemanly fingers around the mug closest to him, brought it to his lips, and blew into it as if to cool a scalding broth. All the while, his gaze never wavered.

Adriani marveled at the level of respect his young student commanded, and the power his demeanor wielded over those around him. *A natural diplomat,* Adriani thought to himself.

The pomegranate juice finally cooled to Niccolò's liking. After swilling it around a few times to further reduce its temperature, he took a judicious sip, stopped a moment to savor it, and set the mug gently back down.

"Should Charles and his men indeed infest our city, I suggest we muster several thousand armed citizens," whispered Niccolò with dispassionate ruthlessness, "and place them at specific vantage points around the city, bell towers, private residences, and rooftops, to counter any potential aggression by the king."

"You do not fear he would trounce on us at the very sight of such resistance?" said Adriani, clearly pleased by Niccolò's patriotic words, but compelled to play devil's advocate.

"The Borgia pope represents his true adversary in this endeavor," said Niccolò. "His thirst for power marks the Vatican as a formidable rival, a concern we share with the French. And of course after completing his adventures in Naples, Charles will have to retrace his steps back through the peninsula." Niccolò locked eyes with Adriani once again to underscore his point. "Therefore, unless the king is a complete fool, he must realize that our friendship will prove quite useful to him."

The following week Niccolò met his Latin professor after his lecture once again at the same tavern. Adriani looked forlorn, his eyes heavy, the congenial smile usually a fixture on his cheerful face gone. Upon seeing Niccolò enter the lecture hall, Adriani had asked him to meet him afterward, almost as if he needed to hear the sober thoughts of a reasonable man to help calm his nerves, or perhaps brighten his spirits. Clearly, on a day like today, pomegranate juice would not fit the bill.

"Bring us two glasses of your most ferociously distilled wine!" Adriani shouted to the craggy old waiter as he hurried past.

Niccolò shook his head. He had never heard an order like that before. "Distilled wine?" he asked innocently.

"Several winters ago in the Veneto, on my travels to La Serenissima," said Adriani with the cadence of one about to recount an old tale, "a gentle farmer welcomed me into his home to spare me from the freezing wind and rain. The fire blazing in the hearth erased the chill from my bones; the singsong of his Venetian dialect soothed me; and his dear wife—a severe woman of few words, I might add—served me a hot supper of cornmeal and broad beans, which went a long way toward easing whatever restlessness I might have harbored during my voyage. But it was the grappa—the vapors squeezed from the seeds, stems, pips, and leaves of their most vintage wine, a liquid as crystalline as a wellspring, and a spirit meant only for the humblest of souls—that lulled me to sleep on that wretched night."

His gaze turned inward; he sat there deep in thought. Niccolò noticed the hint of a smile come and go on his professor's lips.

Adriani finally pointed to a rickety wooden door in the dark corner of the tavern, the entrance to a cantina. "The proprietor of this respectable establishment keeps bottles of just such a spirit in his cellar for sad occasions like this one."

The old waiter brought a wooden tray of *crostini* smeared with goose liver, garlic, and olive oil to fill their bellies. Florentine custom dictated that no liquor of such potency should be drunk on an empty stomach. This included wine, sherry, and Florence's own Vin Santo, which would rarely be consumed without the requisite hazelnut-filled biscuits. Niccolò wasted no time in picking up the crostino piled with the most paté and topped with the most amount of oil, and chomped right into it. Despite his lean frame, Niccolò's appetite, in all matters large or small, was nothing short of insatiable.

"Sad occasion?" repeated Niccolò.

Adriani smiled awkwardly, obviously not yet prepared to address the subject. He helped himself to a crostino, and fortunately for him, the waiter finally arrived with their grappa. He took a quick, deliberate sip, letting the heat of its high-potency alcohol settle his nerves as well as provide him the courage to speak.

"The friar has arranged for representatives of the French king to march into our city where they will choose the homes and establishments suitable for the king and his vast contingent of men."

Niccolò, who had just taken another bite of his crostino, continued chewing nonchalantly, trying his best to hide his rising sense of disgust. His face betrayed no feeling one way or another. He decided instead to wait for a further explanation before offering an opinion.

Adriani kindly obliged. "The friar has acquiesced to the king's demands, plain and simple."

"To occupy our homes?" asked Niccolò flatly.

It took a moment before Adriani could finally nod in the affirmative. He, like all loyal and patriotic Florentine citizens, could not bear the thought of such a dishonor. At this point, Niccolò lost all control.

"Our homes?" he roared. "And just how will these homes be chosen?"

"The front doors of all buildings intended to host the French king, his servants, and his men will be marked with chalk," said Adriani in a voice so subdued it could hardly be discerned.

"Can we as a people be so easily conquered?" cried Niccolò. "With simple sticks of chalk?"

As if on cue, a rumbling at the tavern's entrance stole everyone's attention. Niccolò, who sat with an obstructed view of the door, bolted to his feet for a better look. A curious and startled Adriani followed suit. Before long, every patron in the tavern turned to witness the commotion. A hushed silence hit the room as the door swung open to reveal five uniformed men gathered outside, clearly French soldiers. One of them, standing resolutely to one side, brandished the coat of arms of Charles VIII, a silk banner with three fleur-de-lys embossed on a sky blue background and quartered with a Jerusalem cross. Two of the men were regular gendarme wearing half-armor and brandishing a light lance, while a fourth man—the commanding officer, judging from the richness of his outfit—wore masses of multihued plumes and an elaborately stitched velvet coat over a layer of meshed armor. He sat atop a fully chainmail-armored horse, his eyes fixed on the fifth man, also a young gendarme, as he scrawled a cross over the door with an unwieldy chunk of limestone.

Niccolò could not speak. His disgust and humiliation had reached a breaking point.

Niccolò's indignation actually didn't hit rock bottom until a few days later. Word had spread throughout Florence that all citizens, no matter their political leanings, family status, or position in society, were to compose themselves with absolute decorum and respect when Charles and his entourage marched through the city gates. Niccolò had managed to calmly extricate himself from the tavern that day without incident, despite the French officer sitting astride his horse declaring the establishment off limits to all Florentines and reserved solely for the troops accompanying the king. Niccolò couldn't, however, promise that same level of self-control today. The unbridled patriotism he felt for his native city triggered emotions that threatened to undermine his usual detached and objective manner. His blood boiled as he watched the arrival of the French into the Piazza del Duomo. The seven huge formations of Swiss soldiers marching at the head of the royal procession with impeccable precision sent pangs of raw anger pulsing through Niccolò like waves of highly charged electricity. The beating of their drums and the piercing timbre of their bagpipes only added insult to injury.

"Remember this day, my friend," remarked Niccolò to Biagio. "The seventeenth of November, 1494, the day our dear city was thrown to the wolves."

Overwhelmed by the pomp and outright arrogance of it all, Biagio stood speechless at Niccolò's side as hundreds of men-at-arms astride caped horses turned the southern corner of via dei Calzaiuoli and filed into the piazza.

"The infighting, intrigue, and betrayal of our Italian neighbors shall be our ruin," said Niccolò, never taking his eyes off the spectacle.

"I imagine they care little for their own integrity," added Biagio, "and even less for that of our peninsula."

"Venice has turned a blind eye, Ferrara took sides with our French invaders, and Bologna has formed an alliance with Milan to undermine our security and freedom," said Niccolò.

"And of course the Borgia pope can be trusted least of all," Biagio was quick to add.

"Our Medici leaders were no better. Before abandoning our city to hide within the alleyways and canals of the Republic of Venice, Piero surrendered the fortresses of Livorno, Pisa, Pietrasanta, Sarzana, Ripafratta, and Sarzanello to that French savage," Niccolò blurted out. "All crucial vantage points for armies filtering in from the North!"

Thousands of foot soldiers and archers followed the men-at-arms, their hard leather soles clapping against the cobblestone in counterpoint to the incessant beating of the drums and whistling of the Swiss pipes. There was no escaping it—the king had planned a grandiose entrance, one whose pure ostentation and vulgarity would establish him as master of the city. Finally, after nearly an hour of parading, Charles VIII appeared atop his elaborately caped steed with his lance at rest, a gesture intended both as a show of peace and as a sign of his confidence in Florentine submission to his authority. To ensure the city's total capitulation, a formidable army marched behind the king. As was to be expected, city magistrates and members of Florence's most respected families met Charles in front of the church of Santa Maria del Fiore to pay homage, and ceremoniously ushered him through its massive doors to commence his benediction.

The crowd that had assembled to witness their own humiliation at the hands of a foreign occupier began to disperse, the shock of the morning's events obvious in their downcast eyes.

After an extended period of stunned silence, frustration, and utter embarrassment, Niccolò turned to Biagio. "I intend to do all I can to stop this humiliation," he said firmly. He and Biagio watched the last of the king's entourage march into the church. "One day soon, Biagio, I shall enter the halls of government, and my work, I promise you, shall be for the good of this city."

Chapter Ten

1513: *THE PRINCE* VS. *DISCOURSES*

Niccolò's voyage back to Sant'Andrea after his adventures in Florence nearly killed him. When La Riccia bid goodbye to Biagio and him at her doorstep, the rain had already flooded the city streets and muddied every inch of the fourteen-kilometer road back home. To make matters worse, the frigid December winds turned the pouring rain into sharp slithers of ice. Biagio did nothing but complain the entire way, and his twenty-year-old horse, Bischero, with its joints aching of arthritis and its one good eye clouded with cataracts, stumbled along at a snail's pace. Bischero's need for constant nourishment required stopping for hay and fresh water in every village or livery stable along their path, and since his teeth had either worn down to nothing or fallen out years ago, each meal seemed to last a lifetime. Of course, Niccolò had routinely weathered similar climactic conditions during his frequent diplomatic trips to the northern territories, especially France and Germany, but his fervent sense of mission and single-minded dedication to resolving the political issues at hand overshadowed whatever hardships he might have suffered. Having to battle the freezing air and gelid downpours of Tuscany for no other reason than to resume a meaningless life in the country gave him no comfort and precious little strength to resist whatever came his way. And, of course, he also wasn't getting any younger.

Marietta had the house ready for them when they shuffled through the door. A piping hot bowl of ceci bean and chicory soup met them as soon as they dried off around the crackling fire. They ate much later than usual due to the long voyage, so they hastened directly into Niccolò's study afterward. Niccolò was anxious to get back to work, and Biagio, too, couldn't wait to dig into his friend's little book and lend a hand or offer a piece of advice wherever he could.

"You have been cursed with excellent calligraphy, my dear Biagio," said Niccolò as they sat around his desk, "which requires you, I am afraid, to transcribe my humble words into legible script once we have finished here."

"It would be my honor," said Biagio, already starting to leaf through a rough copy of *The Prince* that was marked with the cover page *De Principatibus*. "Is this everything?" he remarked, noting its modest length.

"Do not be fooled by its brevity. Each page represents years of study and decades of true experience."

"You don't have to tell me. Lest you forget, I've been at your side for—"

"Twenty years. Yes, I know, Biagio," said Niccolò, teasing his old friend.

"Since the very day you made your grand decision to become a civil servant," Biagio added, rubbing it in.

"An ignominious day," said Niccolò, deciding to bring the

discussion back to some semblance of seriousness. "Not because of my decision, of course. I am grateful and fortunate to have had the opportunity to serve my city."

"Then it must be because I stayed at your side," quipped Biagio.

"That too," said Niccolò in jest. "But if I may be serious a moment . . . the shame we had to suffer at the hands of that French brute still sticks in my craw."

"But we stood our ground in the end. And willing to die to keep our city free."

"We can thank our chief officer, Piero Capponi, for that. The rumor still swirls throughout the territories that he single-handedly stopped the reentry of the Medici into our city."

"I believe Savonarola took credit for that piece of diplomacy," countered Biagio.

"It is true that the friar and Capponi arranged a meeting with Charles to frame a treaty, but the king's insistence on Piero de' Medici's return had Capponi quivering with rage," said Niccolò. "Adriani brought me with him to visit the poor man on his deathbed two years later. Capponi told me of his actions on that day with great detail and the pride of a true Florentine."

"It was also his idea to arm our citizenry, was it not?" added Biagio. "Then place them strategically around the city to counter any false moves by the French."

"Six thousand men in all," said Niccolò with a sly grin, remembering all too well his advice to Adriani in the tavern to do the very same thing. "There can be no lasting truce without the teeth to support it."

"Remind me, then, never to sign a truce with my horse," joked Biagio.

Niccolò tried hard to stifle a smile. He knew better than to indulge his old friend in these situations. Biagio shrugged as if to say, "Sorry, I can't help myself," and, as always, Niccolò went right back to his explanation.

"The king's outrageous demands, and in particular his boundless arrogance, angered Capponi so much that he grabbed the treaty they had just signed and tore it in two," said Niccolò. "And as the king sat there, open-mouthed, literally stunned into silence, we proclaimed our readiness to do battle if necessary. 'You sound your trumpets and we will sound our bells!' Capponi cried."

"Did that French idiot even know what that meant?" asked Biagio.

Niccolò laughed. "The French know about war, but they know little of the subtlety of politics. Capponi played his hand quite well."

"Charles had already seen our men stationed throughout the city, armed and ready to ruffle his feathers, when he entered our gates," said Biagio.

"And he was in no mood to fight," Niccolò added. "Capponi perceived that immediately. When the king finally left two weeks later and marched toward Siena, he found himself one hundred and twenty thousand florins richer."

"Quite the ransom."

"And of course since Charles couldn't get his way regarding his demand to bring the Medici back, he had his men rummage through their palaces to take whatever they could find," said Niccolò with a smirk, recalling how the people of Florence expressed pure joy when they heard that bit of news.

"To rid ourselves of the French as well as the Medici in one fell swoop was almost too good to be true," Biagio added.

"Savonarola's threats of divine wrath if Charles overstayed

his welcome helped expedite matters," said Niccolò. "The friar's reputation as a man of great independence, who regarded himself as a prophet sent by God to reform the Church, had spread to all the courts of Europe. He came to redeem all of Italy! Charles was not only a practical man, but a Christian of deep faith as well. His artillery may have been able to blast through impregnable city walls, and his armies vastly outnumbered ours, but he had no interest in testing the legitimacy of Savonarola's status as a messenger of God."

"Our homely, unwashed, and pock-marked little Frenchman was more than happy to get out of Florence," said Biagio, laughing out loud.

"And once he was out of our hair, we could get down to the business I was born for," said Niccolò.

"And what might that be?"

"Helping to form a free republic."

"You were never one to exaggerate, Machia; why should you start now?" remarked Biagio. "Twenty years ago, when the new Republic was created, you and I were too busy roaming the streets of San Frediano to partake in such grave endeavors as forming a republic."

"While you slept into the early afternoons I accompanied Adriani to meetings with members of the Signoria to discuss that very thing," said Niccolò. "Why do you think they chose me for the Second Chancery?"

Biagio reached over and picked up Niccolò's treatise. "Yet I sit here holding a book you have written—and have asked me to review, I might add—on the nature of princes and principalities, not republics. Am I confused or are you indeed celebrating the complete *opposite* of a free republic within these pages?"

"You speak ad nauseam of being at my side for all these

many years, but it seems you still do not know me," countered Niccolò. "I have already begun to expound on the three forms of 'good' government in my *Discourses*: monarchy, principality, and a democratic republic, and of course I tout the last as being superior to all others!"

Realizing he had bruised his friend's integrity, Biagio quickly replied, "I surely did not mean to imply—"

"Liberty must be guarded and protected," interjected Niccolò, eager to set his friend straight, "and it ought to be done by the people. They have the least desire of usurping it! I harbor disparaging words for Savonarola and his regime throughout my writings, it is true, but once again I give credit where credit is due. The friar's influence on forming the charters of our free Republic in those early days after Charles's departure proved instrumental. I can attest to that."

"If I remember correctly, you had a few choice words in opposition to those charters back then," said Biagio.

"Of course I did!" Niccolò shot back at the top of his lungs. "Calumny ran rampant, insults flew with reckless abandon, and lifelong grudges between families corroded the moral fabric of the city! This could not go on unchecked!"

Biagio tried to defuse the ire he'd aroused in his old friend by offering a few kind words, but Niccolò wanted no part of it. He had apparently not finished his tirade.

"The new government failed to create a justice system where citizens had the liberty to denounce others or defend themselves without fear or suspicion. Falsehoods continued to go unpunished, and scandals, the scourge of our dear city, proceeded to sabotage our freedoms."

"Are you finished?" Biagio asked a bit sheepishly, but not without plenty of sarcasm.

Niccolò cleared his throat, evidently somewhat embarrassed by his little outburst.

Biagio took advantage of the pause. "Is this concerning La Riccia, may I ask?"

"La Riccia? What are you talking about?"

"Your anger. I suspect it is because of my feelings for La Riccia."

"Don't be a fool. I am content when she lets me steal a kiss from her," said Niccolò. "So, let it be known that I am quite content."

"Then Vettori, perhaps?" said Biagio.

"Vettori? What do you take me for? I would never allow that scoundrel to kiss me," quipped Niccolò.

Biagio burst out laughing. Once again, he got caught off guard by "il Machia." But as innocuous as Niccolò's reaction seemed, it demonstrated his uncanny ability to mix the ridiculous with the sublime. He could shift moods at the drop of a hat, and win friends or stifle enemies with the turn of a phrase, all without compromising his integrity. Sure, he might have allowed a bit of anger to rear its ugly head over La Riccia, but he was born with plenty of common sense and lightheartedness, and had acquired enough mindfulness and nonchalance over his lifetime to field any question, reciprocate any compliment, or counter any insult with just enough sincerity—or artifice, if necessary—to achieve the desired result.

"Perhaps you are right," admitted Niccolò. "Vettori never responds to my pleas for help without incessant prodding."

"Have you ever thought of why he still has the ear of our Medici rulers in Florence while you languish here in the country?" said Biagio. "And how it is that his influence still carries weight within the walls of the Vatican?" He shook his head in dismay. "Be careful. The man plays his cards very close to his chest."

Niccolò nodded. "I'm afraid any future services I shall provide for our dear city will be limited to my work as a vendor of firewood."

"That may be better than working for these new Medici lords, which you somehow hope to do by dedicating this little book to them."

"I need to use my talents where they can be of help."

"They threw you in prison and accused you of crimes beneath your dignity the moment they got back into power!" cried Biagio.

"Allow me to remind you that Leo X, a Medici pope, set me free," Niccolò replied.

"And forced you to abandon the city of your birth!"

"Am I angry? Yes, I am, and I would like nothing more than revenge. But things come and go, Biagio my friend," said Niccolò. "Man is a victim of nature's forces and subjected to the whims of Fortune. My readings of Lucretius have taught me that, and his ideas have guided my hand while writing both *The Prince* and *Discourses* alike. We were able to chase out the Medici in '94 due in part to the virtues of great men, and in part to the capriciousness of Fortune. We enjoyed many years of self-rule. That disappeared one short year ago when a different combination of Virtue and Fortune ushered the Medici back into our lives. But there are greater forces that confront us from beyond the borders of our peninsula. Perhaps I can help our Medici rulers resist those forces. What else can I do?"

"When you say 'Virtue,' I assume you do not imply the Christian virtues."

"Faith, hope, and love are of little consequence when confronted with hard steel."

"I may have been cursed with fine calligraphy, as you say, but you, my friend, are doomed to see the world as it really is," said Biagio, "and not as we would like it to be."

"Exactly the words I use in that little book," said Niccolò, pointing to his manuscript of *The Prince* gripped firmly in Biagio's hands.

Biagio looked him straight in the eye. "Why offer your talents to a tyrannical Medici regime when your writings will outlive you, and your words will endure long after you're gone?" he asked. "You have shared a table with warring kings, ambitious princes, and shrewd diplomats. Even hostile and corrupt popes know they have met their match in you. Louis XII of France, Maximilian of Hapsburg, Cesare Borgia, Caterina Sforza, Julius II—they have all seen you up close. They know you, and what you are made of. They have felt your wisdom; your words have calmed their aggressions, appeased their desires, even enlightened them as to the ways of good governance, all while safeguarding the peace of our city and the welfare of our citizens. We depended on your comprehensive reports and words of advice for fourteen years. I believe it's time you share them with future generations, and what better place for those words to flourish than within the covers of a book? That is what you can do!"

Niccolò sat in silence a moment, moved by Biagio's tribute, then signaled his appreciation with a nod. "And that is exactly what I am doing," he said.

"Why not, then, place all your time and expertise on finishing this book you call your *Discourses,* which deals with the formation of a true and lasting republic?"

"Allow me first to conclude our discussion on the friar's influence on our free republic."

"That was your discussion, Machia, not mine," countered Biagio. "My question to you is of a different nature."

"As I was saying," Niccolò shot back, the touch of annoyance in his voice tempered with a smile, "despite my biting words concerning the self-destruction of Florence at the hands of scandalmongers and warring families, I have nothing but praise for the Republic formed under Savonarola's tutelage. It was, after all, except for a few alterations here and there, the very same form of government to which I would later pledge my allegiance as second secretary. But you know as well as I that what Italy needs now is a strong leader, a prince if need be, to unite us against our foreign invaders."

"You once told me you never felt more proud to be a Florentine than when the bells rang out in the Palazzo Vecchio after Charles's departure," said Biagio. "The bells of a free republic!"

"But there can be no lasting freedom for our beloved Florence while we remain divided against the very states that threaten that freedom," said Niccolò. "Our Signoria, with its gonfalonier and eight priori, is a symbol of liberty. We endeavored to preserve that institution during our general parliament the moment Charles left our city. We kept the Magistracy of the Eight, and the Magistracy of the Ten of War as well. We should be proud."

"Then why not write about it and preserve it in our memory?" insisted Biagio.

"The formation of the Great Council put forward by Savonarola was a masterstroke," said Niccolò. "It gave all citizens the opportunity to participate in government, which, Biagio my friend, is the key to good democracy. But as we know, these institutions need our constant vigilance to survive, and when the time comes, I fully intend to discuss all of this, and more, in my *Discourses*."

Biagio got up to stoke the fire while Niccolò went on about the Great Council's responsibilities of appointing city magistrates, approving or rejecting laws put forward by the Signoria, overseeing voting regulations, and electing the Council of Eighty, who then appointed commissioners and ambassadors. The more Niccolò explained the workings of Savonarola's brainchild, the more the joyous story of the Republic's birth brought the tragedy of the friar's eventual demise into stark relief.

"Unfortunately for Savonarola, in the end his God abandoned him," said Biagio.

Niccolò picked up his manuscript of *The Prince* and paged through it until he found what he was looking for. He cleared his throat, then read aloud: "Thus it comes to pass that all armed prophets have conquered and all unarmed ones have failed."

Chapter Eleven

1498: THE SECOND CHANCERY

Four years had passed since King Charles VIII's abrupt exit from the city of Florence. On the morning of the twenty-second of May, 1498, Niccolò, now twenty-nine and in the prime of his life, stood among thousands of his fellow citizens in the Piazza della Signoria waiting for yet another drama in the city's history to unfold. As the anticipation grew, he couldn't help but think back on the events that had brought him, and his beloved Florence, to this unfortunate crossroad. He recalled Charles's eventual takeover of the Kingdom of Naples, and how in typical fashion all the city-states of Italy openly congratulated their foreign conqueror while secretly plotting their resistance: The harsh reality of such a powerful figure occupying a major portion of the peninsula quickly began to take hold. Rather than awaken a sense of unity among the city-states, however, the French presence set fire to their petty fears, provoking infighting and fierce political maneuvering. The Most Serene Republic of Venice grew nervous seeing its commercial superiority on the peninsula challenged; Pisa and Siena, bolstered by French support, broke away from Florence, severely enfeebling the city's economy; and Florence itself was thrown into disarray.

Once Charles retraced his steps and abandoned the peninsula without major incident, leaving governors in Naples to look after his newly acquired kingdom, Florence found itself deprived of a valuable ally, thus weakening its stability. As a result, Friar Savonarola gained more power, and his righteousness grew increasingly strident and unforgiving. His theocratic democracy took firm root. The problem of widespread corruption that had long been eroding the city's moral fiber, and which Savonarola had promised to eradicate, was supplanted by a reign of terror. The humanist tradition that formed the intellectual and cultural backdrop of the Republic faded into the background, or, more precisely, went underground.

The crowd in the piazza grew increasingly anxious as they waited for the main event to begin. Cries of "Retribution!" echoed off the stone walls of the Palazzo Vecchio and the Loggia dei Lanzi, Florence's architectural symbol of the Republic. As Niccolò looked out over the hordes of angry and vengeful citizens, his gaze fixed on an ominous bronze statue on the steps of the palazzo. The citizens of Florence had transported this eight-foot statue of Judith and Holofernes just four years ago from the Medici palace to the Piazza della Signoria to celebrate their ouster. The selection of this particular work by their native artist, Donatello, of a young woman beheading a powerful despot did not happen by chance, and its symbolism of the people's victory over tyranny couldn't be more poignant.

With the Medici gone and the new Republic beginning to take hold, the future seemed bright for the city of Florence. But as time passed, Savonarola's moralism, undue austerity, and fiery rhetoric ate away at the Republic's very core. His threats of an imminent apocalypse were increasingly coupled with accusations of corruption and immorality hurled at the Roman Curia. Convinced that God had chosen him to set Florence back on the straight and narrow, Savonarola continued his attacks on the Church. His followers increased, but so did his adversaries. The episode that Niccolò believed eroded the friar's popularity perhaps more than any other was his refusal to uphold a law that he himself had proposed. It involved five prominent Florentine citizens accused of conspiring against the government. Savonarola broke one of Niccolò's cardinal rules: Never make a law that cannot be kept. It is the worst example a ruler can set; it damages his reputation and exposes him to condemnation.

Niccolò's attention was suddenly jolted away from Judith and Holofernes when Savonarola emerged from the Palazzo Vecchio. The crowd exploded with taunts and cries of ridicule. Two fellow Dominicans stood at the friar's side. The hands of all three men were bound behind their backs as papal guards ushered them onto a wooden plank leading to the center of the piazza, where a scaffold, built high atop a pile of tree trunks and severed branches, awaited them. Niccolò couldn't get over the strange sensation of seeing Savonarola's spirit so profoundly deflated. The man he saw shuffling toward the gallows stood in stark contrast to the fiery preacher who delivered deeply passionate sermons before thousands of enthralled devotees each week in the church of San Marco.

However, all of this did not come as a complete surprise to Niccolò, either. He had long predicted a tragic ending to the friar's story. He noticed, for instance, that as the weeks and months passed, Savonarola's indictments against the Church's corruption grew increasingly more strident, aimed directly against Pope Alexander VI himself. *These outbursts will only serve to force the Borgia pope's hand,* Niccolò thought to himself at the time. And of course they eventually did. Alexander called for Savonarola to discontinue his inflammatory sermons, but the friar refused, proclaiming that he only answered to God. He then proceeded to call Alexander the anti-Christ, and exhorted his congregation to abandon any allegiance to the pope, and answer directly to him. Alexander responded by playing his most lethal card: He excommunicated the friar point blank.

Unfazed by the pope's drastic action, Savonarola had letters mailed to all the Italian states accusing Alexander of simony and other egregious sins, imploring them to denounce Alexander as their pontiff. At that point, Alexander, realizing his threats could not alter the friar's resolve, abandoned the hard line and gave way to sheer cunning and trickery, which were always his strongest points. He offered Savonarola a cardinalship on the condition that he travel to Rome to discuss the matter in person. Of course, Alexander's plan was, no doubt, to imprison the friar the moment he set foot on Vatican soil and charge him with heresy. Being no man's fool, however, Savonarola refused the pope's proposal.

In a last-ditch effort to prove his direct connection to God, Savonarola composed his *Triumph of the Cross,* a treatise in which he hinted at his ability to perform miracles. Ironically, it was another monastic order, the Franciscans, that sealed the friar's fate. He was challenged to a trial by fire, an outdated ritual that hadn't been practiced in more than four hundred years. Surviving the fire would substantiate his claims. Savonarola had no choice but to accept. As it turned out, Niccolò, his father, and a horde of curious citizens had gathered in this same piazza just last month to watch these two rival monastic orders vie for religious preeminence over the city. Fortunately for everyone involved, a sudden storm doused the flames of the ritual fire, ending the proceedings. Considering Savonarola to be the loser by default as well as an outright imposter, the crowd assaulted his convent of San Marco. The friar and two fellow Dominicans were carried out, arrested, and thrown into prison, where under pains of torture Savonarola confessed to having fabricated everything: the visions, the prophesies, and the direct line to God, all for the purpose of self-aggrandizement and power. Shortly thereafter, the three Dominican friars were condemned to death as heretics.

A hush befell the crowd as, one by one, the three Dominicans took their place on the scaffold where the executioner, an obese monster of a man, fastened a noose firmly around their necks. All eyes were on Savonarola, who stood silent, indicating neither his innocence nor his guilt, a man dispossessed of all vigor and all power. He issued no warnings, no appeals, no doomsday prophesies, but rather remained stone-faced, unmoved, as the executioner hoisted the first Dominican friar into the air and high above the pile of wood that was suddenly set ablaze. The rope tightened around the friar's throat, instantly blocking his flow of air. Rather than aim at snapping the victim's neck, which would result in a relatively quick, albeit painful, death, the object here was to inflict a long, torturous strangulation followed by a traditional, and infinitely more purifying, burning at the stake. The second friar suffered the same fate. Savonarola, meanwhile, refused to show any emotion, even as the jeers and insults from the crowd grew to a deafening pitch.

Niccolò studied the friar's behavior, noting his every movement. In fact, he'd been monitoring the friar's actions since his entrance into the city nearly ten years ago from his native city of Ferrara. He observed the friar's impact on the people of Florence, the vehement reaction of his detractors, and ultimately the friar's inability to overcome the hostile forces piling up against him. And as he watched the executioner pull the rope that hoisted the friar up and over the burning pyre, the noose taut around his neck, Niccolò's political mind began to process all the events surrounding Girolamo Savonarola's fall from grace right up to his imprisonment, torture, and the violent execution now taking place right before his eyes. So many lasting lessons on how to effectively govern a state suddenly became clear as day. Savonarola's body, along with his two fellow Dominicans, twisted helplessly in the fire. Their screams of agony, muted by the tightening of the noose, converged with the crackling of the burning wood to produce a strange and hellish requiem until they were all consumed by the flames rising beneath them.

Niccolò stayed until the bitter end. Hours later when the last embers released their final plumes of smoke and the crowd had dispersed, Niccolò, one of just a handful of bystanders still left in the piazza, noticed two workers for the government of Florence and a representative of the papal court approach what remained of the scaffold and the bodies that lay in the ashes. The papal representative split off from the other two. He carried a large terra cotta pot into which he began placing pieces of ash and crumbled bone of what was discerned to be Savonarola's remains.

"What do you intend to do with that?" asked Niccolò.

The papal representative, a clergyman with the air of a soldier more than of a man of the Church, shot Niccolò a look of pure contempt, as if to say, "And who in bloody hell are you?"

Niccolò couldn't take his eyes off the scars crisscrossing his weather-worn face. Battle scars, no doubt. It didn't take long for

Niccolò to figure out that Alexander had staged this entire spectacle for his own benefit, and that the government of Florence, although quite willing to put the reign of Savonarola behind it, played second fiddle at best. The Vatican had won a great victory and wanted everyone to know that the Pope of Rome still controlled the hearts and minds of those calling themselves Christians. There would be no schism, no mutiny, no anti-pope, no pretender to the papal throne, and no one else to obey except the duly ordained Pontiff of the Holy Catholic Church of Rome, Pope Alexander VI.

Niccolò did not relent. His steady glare into the clergyman's eyes spoke volumes: Niccolò was not to be taken lightly. The clergyman still decided not to respond. He went back to gathering the powdery remains of the friar's body and tossing them into the terra cotta pot.

"What do you intend to do with the ashes?" insisted Niccolò.

One of the workers for the Florentine government, a lowly operative, lifted his gaze from the work at hand and turned to Niccolò. His job evidently consisted of simply cleaning up the mess, which included throwing the ashes of the other two friars in with all the extinguished coals, embers, and general remains of the fire.

"This all gets carted to the refuse pile under the Ponte di Rubaconte," he said matter-of-factly. "Care to help?" he added with a smirk. He and his government co-worker chuckled under their breath and went back to work.

"And the remains of the man who led our fair city for the past four years—what is to become of him?" asked Niccolò a bit indignantly.

"He will not find sanctuary in the convent of San Marco, if

that is what you intend," said the clergyman. "He will receive the respect all heretics deserve."

"I ask as a free citizen of the Republic of Florence," said Niccolò.

"As well as a Christian under the patronage of Our Holy Mother the Church, one would presume," proclaimed the clergyman.

Niccolò hesitated, then allowed a warm smile to surface. "Of course," he said, sensing that a less aggressive tack would produce more fruitful results.

For a moment it appeared as though the clergyman would volunteer an honest answer, but then he thought better of it. He bent down and returned to his job. Then, perhaps seeing that Niccolò had no intention of pushing the discussion further, he mumbled, "Into the river."

"Excuse me?" said Niccolò, pretending not to hear.

"His remains will be dispersed into the Arno," said the clergyman.

Niccolò expected that very answer. He knew that Pope Alexander's greatest fear after disposing of Savonarola and the threat he posed to the hegemony of the Church was seeing him catapulted to the status of martyr. Any portion of him, whether it be a fragment of bone, a sliver of fingernail, or even a single strand of his garment, could become a valuable relic for devotees to worship, for churches to attract pilgrims, or for zealots and political enemies of the Church to rally around. It was at that moment that Niccolò realized that Savonarola had been roundly defeated. Unlike Moses, an "armed prophet" who perhaps more than any religious figure in history satisfied Niccolò's rigid criteria for true political success, Savonarola erroneously believed that his righteousness and special bond with God constituted the only virtues he needed to achieve his goals.

The folly of that mode of thinking crystallized for Niccolò right then and there. Savonarola possessed no real means of keeping those who believed in him, or of compelling his skeptics to join him. Words without the resources to back them up were worthless in the political sphere. Careful readings of ancient history had prepared Niccolò well to comprehend the import of Savonarola's unhappy ending. Without uttering another word, Niccolò walked away.

A short time later Niccolò walked up the wide marble steps in the Palazzo Vecchio to the second floor. He had been visited by a messenger several days earlier at his home on via Guicciardini with a note from Marcello Adriani to meet him in his office. Adriani had succeeded Bartolomeo Scala as Florence's chancellor after his death late in 1497, and over the past few months Niccolò had been called in to help on various day-to-day affairs, so his presence in the halls of the grand palazzo took no one by surprise. *God only knows what menial task the good chancellor has in store for me today,* Niccolò thought to himself. Adriani retained his professorship in Letters at the University of Florence while performing his role as chancellor, as was customary, and would often meet with Niccolò after his lectures to discuss political matters as they did years earlier when Niccolò frequented the university.

Niccolò walked down a long corridor and stopped in front of a set of massive double doors. He knocked lightly, then opened them and walked right in without waiting for someone to beckon him inside. Adriani was sitting idly, staring into space, when Niccolò entered the room. The chancellor didn't budge, still lost in thought even as Niccolò approached his desk and took a seat across from him.

The events of earlier that day overwhelmed Adriani. His involvement in Savonarola's execution, under the stern direction of the Vatican, no doubt, had been preoccupying him and his office for weeks, even months. The long days of torture inflicted on the friar at the hands of the government, the very government Savonarola had served for the past four years, followed by a steady routine of torture, then his eventual confession—perhaps issued under duress—and a guilty verdict handed out just yesterday morning . . . all of it had taken its toll on Adriani's already frazzled nerves. Certainly a part of him breathed a sigh of relief to finally be rid of such a disturbing and unpredictable force. At least when the Medici ruled the city, their machinations were hidden from public view, conjured up behind closed doors, and certainly not promulgated from the pulpit, or forced down people's throats by zealots or political opportunists. Perhaps most importantly, by doing away with the friar, the city managed to avoid being placed under interdict by a vengeful and sadistic pope, an action that would have severely damaged Florence's economic and social standing. Yet, to subject the populous to such an emotional trauma, to carry out a spectacle of this savagery—especially one so obviously orchestrated by the Vatican—would undoubtedly leave a lasting scar on the city. And all this happening so early in Adriani's tenure as chancellor could only be viewed as a political blow to his authority. He needed to do something about it. *Florence had to assert itself better on the political stage,* he told himself on a near-daily basis. It was his duty to make it happen.

Finally, as if he'd awakened from a bad dream, Adriani

turned to his former student and welcomed him with a friendly nod. "How's the family?"

"The same, I suppose," said Niccolò. "My sisters do most of the cleaning and cooking since my poor mother passed away. It's no wonder they're miserable. And Totto tells them every day how much he hates their cooking."

"And your father?"

"He hates their cooking as well," quipped Niccolò.

Adriani shifted in his seat. Niccolò's wit and dry, gallows humor always caught him off guard. "I meant how's your father doing?"

"We have become even closer," said Niccolò. "He asks me every day if I've heard anything concerning the position in the Second Chancery."

"Did you tell him there are three other very qualified applicants?" asked Adriani a bit mischievously.

"I also tell him it is still quite early in the process," said Niccolò, forcing a smile, "and they haven't made up their minds just yet."

Adriani nodded his head, and being a prudent man, he chose not to shed any further light on the topic for the moment. He was only five years older than Niccolò, but had the demeanor of someone twice his age. Adriani had already accomplished much in life; his family's status in the city afforded him every opportunity to succeed. Niccolò, on the other hand, had not yet been given the chance to prove himself, but instilled confidence in everyone he met. The veneer of respectability covered them both from head to toe—Adriani for his position in government, level of sophistication, and formality of manner, and Niccolò for his insight, candor, and nimbleness of mind. When it came to affairs of state, their goals coincided. They saw eye to eye on most of the important issues, and their respect for one another made for a formidable team. But Adriani affected the posture of a much more traditional and conservative man, and Niccolò treated him as such. Their relationship, therefore, could never rise above the professional level or dig any deeper into personal or emotional issues. The distance between them was marked by a yawning gap in their social standing that simply could not be changed.

Niccolò knew this all too well. He also knew, as did Adriani, that he had great potential as a government leader and administrator, but the Second Chancery, although an extremely important and influential position, was the best he could hope for, given his place in society.

After an awkward silence, Adriani sat up straight in his chair. "What if I were to tell you we have already made our decision?"

"Oh," said Niccolò, remaining calm and collected. "And?"

Adriani allowed a slight grin to form. Niccolò couldn't tell, however, whether it was a sign of good news or a diplomatic ruse for communicating quite the opposite.

"As you most obviously are aware of, the position is an important one," Adriani said.

"Indeed it is," replied Niccolò, holding back a grin of his own. *This man enjoys watching me squirm,* he thought to himself while finally allowing a smile to emerge.

Niccolò was well acquainted with the importance of the job. Three very complex and delicate orders of business fell under Florence's purview. Most informed citizens could tell you that. The first involved the city's internal affairs. Florence was, after all, a thriving, self-determining commune. The second order of business consisted of supervising the vast Tuscan territories that included expansive rural lands and a good number of proud, freedom-loving, and often-contentious cities such as Pisa, Arezzo, Prato, and Pistoia. And last, as a sovereign power on the Italian peninsula, Florence had to deal independently with neighboring states and foreign monarchs.

"Although the decision has been made, the final confirmation will come as late as next month," said Adriani, continuing his delaying tactic.

"I assume, however, since you have called me here today, that you have something to tell me," said Niccolò.

"Or perhaps to give you more work to do," said Adriani. "This is quite the busy time, wouldn't you say? It's not every day we execute a political leader, man of God, and heretic," he added, affecting a smile.

Niccolò said nothing. He allowed Adriani a moment to throw some light on his last few words or perhaps add a personal note. Adriani, too, waited. He sat back in his chair, then fixed his gaze on Niccolò, which to Niccolò appeared as if Adriani were sizing him up.

"What exactly do you think the job at the Second Chancery entails, should we decide to offer you the position?" asked Adriani, donning his chancellor hat, a trait he rarely exhibited when chatting with his former student. "I ask because whoever occupies the role may also serve as secretary to the chancellor."

"That would further expand the responsibilities of the secretary of the Second Chancery to include service in the Ten of War," said Niccolò, "which would consist of overseeing foreign affairs and diplomacy." He gave it some more thought, then added: "To a certain extent, it would combine the duties of the War Office and the Ministry for Internal Affairs."

"And are you sure you understand what that means?" asked Adriani.

Niccolò didn't hesitate in answering: "In addition to the regular task of handling the correspondence that relates to the administration of our territories, which is an integral part of the second secretary's duties, the secretary may also be asked to travel beyond the walls of his office, his city, or even the Florentine territories."

"Where, as the city's ambassador, he will meet with diplomats and heads of state, and relay important and detailed assessments back to the chancellor and Signoria," Adriani was quick to add.

"In essence, the two chanceries would merge under the leadership of the chancellor," said Niccolò.

Adriani nodded in agreement. "France, Spain, the Hapsburgs in Germany, and even Rome or Milan would require being away from home for weeks, if not months, at a time."

Niccolò bowed his head ever so slightly in reverence. "To serve the city of Florence in whatever capacity would be a great honor, Magnificent Chancellor, should the position go to me."

Adriani straightened up in his chair, quite satisfied. "Is it true you are soon to be betrothed?" he asked, affecting a decidedly lighter tone.

Niccolò's demeanor did not alter one bit. He fielded the question exactly how it was intended—that is to say as an inquiry into his willingness to be away from family and friends for extended periods.

"I have spoken to Marietta and her family about it," Niccolò said. "They would be honored as well to make whatever sacrifices are necessary for the welfare of the Republic."

Adriani dropped the façade. He rose from his chair. Out of deference, Niccolò did the same. The two men stood across from each other, several feet apart, their eyes fixed straight ahead, silent, each respectful of the other, each eager to get to the point. Adriani finally broke the ice.

"The committee has chosen you for the position, Signor Machiavelli."

Niccolò's thin lips formed an impish smile that betrayed both a sense of sincere appreciation and a playful look that said *Of course, who else could it have been?* The two men locked into a warm, manly hug.

Chapter Twelve

1513: MY LITTLE BOOK

Niccolò and Biagio tiptoed around their assigned project of reading Niccolò's little book for over an hour. They talked instead about everything else under the sun. But at last things started to settle down. Desiccated olive branches crackled in the fireplace, robbing the moist chill from the air, and Niccolò had finally exhausted every piece of political minutiae that crossed his mind. For his part, Biagio couldn't help but jump from topic to topic as well, as he was wont to do, but the mental chaos soon dissipated and the chatter finally came to a standstill. The rain continued to do its damage outside, and their after-dinner glass of Vin Santo had begun fulfilling its job of digesting the ceci bean soup Marietta had prepared for them. For all intents and purposes they were ready to get down to business. Biagio unfurled several sheets of the manuscript until arriving at the page labeled "Chapter One."

Niccolò stood by the fire, staring at the glowing embers, allowing himself to be mesmerized by them as he so often did when he needed to free his mind or find needed inspiration. He had read his rough copy of *The Prince* dozens of times to himself, as well as aloud, but to hear his thoughts echoed in the hallowed chambers of his study by a foreign voice—someone reading it for the first time, who could no doubt catch even the most casual error in grammar, awkward turn of phrase, or, heaven forbid, a line of ill-conceived logic—filled him with more anxiety than he ever expected.

Truth be told, Biagio was absolutely certain that he would find no syntactical missteps or flaws in Niccolò's reasoning; he knew his friend too well for that. After all, they had corresponded scores of times over the past fourteen years in the Chancery. Niccolò had written literally hundreds of missives to foreign dignitaries and members of the Signoria ranging from intricate descriptions of a chief of state's frame of mind to personal judgments on highly sensitive political matters to long, detailed accounts of daily events. Biagio carried a lot of weight in the Chancery as well, and was relied upon to transmit and receive important information to and from ranking members of the Signoria as well as to Florence's ambassadors in the field. Both men possessed a fine-tuned ear for a clever figure of speech or an exalted piece of reasoning, but Biagio knew he could never compete with Niccolò's rhetorical skills, mental acuity, or uncanny insights into the psyches of powerful men.

What stirred up more than a good amount of apprehension in Biagio was the thought of coming face-to-face with material in this little book that proved too erudite or nuanced to fully comprehend. He cherished the fact that Niccolò had full confidence in him. What greater compliment could there be? And of course he didn't want to let his friend down or fall short of his expectations, so he began his reading of the book by enunciating each word slowly and deliberately so as to not miss a thing.

"Chapter One," he read in a firm voice, "the various kinds of governments and the ways in which they are established." He stopped and peered over at Niccolò, whose gaze remained glued to the fire and whose ears hung on Biagio's every syllable.

"Is that it? Have you finished already?" said Niccolò, doing nothing to hide his impatience.

"Didn't you say you wanted to dedicate the book to Lorenzo?" Biagio asked.

"I will compose the dedication in due time. For what it's worth, I will wait for Vettori's suggestions," said Niccolò. "Now, will you please get on with it?"

Biagio cleared his throat. The opening lines of this brief chapter delineated two essential types of states—monarchies and republics—how they are acquired, and how they are maintained. As Biagio droned on, Niccolò stoked the fire to the beat of each word. The subsequent paragraphs described the makeup of these states in common rhetorical terms. Nothing out of the ordinary. But when Biagio approached the end of the chapter, the pitch of his voice lifted slightly: "And these dominions can be annexed either by force of arms of the prince himself, or of others, or else they may fall to him by Fortune or Virtue."

Noticing the change in Biagio's tone, Niccolò shifted his attention away from the rising flames of the fire and turned to his friend, expecting to hear more.

"Beautiful," said Biagio sheepishly.

Niccolò tried hard to wipe any sign of condescension from his face. Instead, he attempted to convey a look of patience, but still Biagio said nothing. Niccolò then affected a shrug as if to say *I'm listening in case you have more to say.*

That worked. Biagio bought a little more time by glancing down at the manuscript to reread the last phrase. He finally asked, "Virtue? What exactly do you mean by that?"

Niccolò's simple answer came across more like a riddle: "A special ability to do what is needed."

Now it was Biagio who wanted more. He waited for Niccolò to expound, which he knew his friend would undoubtedly do sooner or later without much insistence.

"To the ancients, Virtue is the talent, or set of talents, that one must possess to attain the ultimate goal of happiness. It was a means unto itself," Niccolò explained. "For the Church, Virtue is the means to eternal happiness in the afterlife. My intention here is somewhat different."

"Are you not interested in the afterlife?" asked Biagio.

"Not if it distracts us from the here and now," Niccolò shot back. "My notion of Virtue combines the energy, courage, prudence, and determination to carry out your plans in this life."

"Of course, one may have an abundance of energy, prudence, courage, and determination, but not a brain in his head and not the slightest idea of how to execute this plan of his."

"Read on, my friend. By the time you reach the final page, you will find that I have explained it all quite well."

"I'll be the judge of that," quipped Biagio.

Niccolò turned back to tending the fire, not so much to ignore Biagio's comment as to hide the smile that spontaneously creased his lips. No one could rival Niccolò's work ethic; it impressed popes and kings alike. He was as serious as a man could be, but laughter was as much a part of life as work. Niccolò lived by that rule.

"And as for Fortune, am I to assume that you include the providence of God in your definition of that word?" asked Biagio.

"The Fortune I speak of is not divine, nor is it preordained or inflexible," said Niccolò. "As for Divine Providence, I cannot presume to address the issue. I shall leave that for the Church to resolve. I focus my principles on what I see, and have seen, unfold before my eyes, as well as on the lessons I have learned from my study of recent and ancient history." Niccolò paused a moment. "For me, Fortune implies that combination of natural forces, seemingly fixed and uncontrollable, that lie outside of us, but have enormous effect on our lives. With proper Virtue we can meet Fortune head-on and bend it to our will."

"So how does prudence, such a temperate virtue, fit in with these other virile traits, if I may ask?" said Biagio.

"Prudence gives you proper foresight into events, which may also mean bending to those events and adapting to them if need be."

"So sometimes a prince must bend Fortune to his will, and sometimes not," said Biagio, a bit of irony in his voice. "I find it simply amazing how you can offer two opposing arguments with such eloquence."

Niccolò was not amused. "Both can be true," he said through gritted teeth. "A skilled prince must know when and how to act on one or the other. Flexibility is a favorable trait and is rarely seen in strong rulers. The fundamental flaw I have noted in leaders that I have met over the years is their inflexibility in the face of changing times. Emperor Maximilian was always overly cautious no matter the circumstances, Julius II too impetuous, and Cesare Borgia lunged forward with perpetual self-confidence." Then, before Biagio could respond, he added: "And I thank you for the compliment."

Biagio sat puzzled for a moment. "Compliment?"

"That I pose my arguments with such eloquence."

Touché. Biagio decided to give Niccolò the last word on this topic by gesturing a tip of the hat, but Niccolò wasn't finished yet: "And I dare say that a fine-tuned diplomat must possess that very same skill."

"Eloquence?" asked Biagio.

"Knowing when to mold Fortune to your benefit, and when to adapt to it," said Niccolò.

Biagio sat back in his X-form folding chair, resting his arms on the side rails for support. He had the sneaking suspicion a further explanation was coming.

"When I first assumed office late in '98, as you can surely remember, we were at war with Pisa."

"Remember? You seem to forget that I have kept a diary of events," Biagio shot back.

"Then you will recall that Venice sent three hundred highly effective, well-armed cavalrymen into the city of Pisa to help defend its walls," said Niccolò. "In addition, not only did its citizens carry arms, but the inhabitants of all the territories in the outlying areas fought proudly and convincingly on Pisa's behalf."

"But it was Venice who presented the real problem," said Biagio.

"I know that!" said Niccolò, exasperated. "Why do you think I'm telling you the story?"

"Actually, I'm not sure," teased Biagio.

Niccolò ignored him and carried on: "During that period, events kept me extremely busy writing to the Signoria regarding the war, forwarding armaments and funds, dispatching orders, and even deliberating with military leaders and foreign dignitaries. But when the Venetians marched into our territories in the Casentino to divert attention and resources away from Pisa, things had gone too far. We were suddenly faced with a conflict on two fronts."

"I must say, you brokered a masterful arbitration between Pisa, Venice, and our dear Republic," said Biagio. "Although the one hundred thousand ducats we agreed to pay the Venetians to quit all hostilities and go home did hurt us in the pocketbook."

"We had to bend to their will in those negotiations," said Niccolò. "It was the wise thing to do, and the only way to continue our fight with the Pisans uninterrupted and eventually bend them to our will—which, of course, is the point of my story."

Biagio took this as a cue to plow ahead. He read through the second chapter on hereditary monarchies without a hitch and breezed into the next chapter on mixed monarchies.

Niccolò threw another log on the fire, pulled up a chair, and sat close enough to the rising flames for the heat to warm his cold fingers. As he listened carefully to his own words being fed to him in measured, clearly pronounced beats, his confidence in the ideas he had put forward grew exponentially. *These are sound precepts,* he thought to himself. *I will surely suffer the wrath of heaven and earth for their bluntness, and for the truths I unveil concerning our political state of affairs, but every true leader who reads my words will recognize the wisdom and practicality of its message.*

Biagio, too, grew increasingly intrigued as he read. "I have seen many of these principles before in Plato and Aristotle," he said, "but never with such candor."

As he continued reading, his voice suddenly registered the same tonal shift as earlier when he came upon a section on how a prince can maintain control over newly acquired territories, specifically the part having to do with people who are not accustomed to living in freedom. Niccolò naturally pricked his ears.

"To possess these states securely, a prince must do two things," read Biagio in a steady voice, "firstly, he must extinguish the family of those who formally governed."

He stopped right there, pausing to reread that passage to himself. Niccolò remained stone-faced, waiting for Biagio's comment. None came. Instead, Biagio read the passage once again, then set the manuscript on the desk. He settled deeper into his seat, adjusting the silk cushion for more comfort, and ran the phrase around in his head one more time.

Anxious to clarify the phrase he knew to be provocative, Niccolò recited the remainder of that sentence from memory: "And secondly, make no alteration in their laws or in their taxes; in this way, in a very short period of time, they will become united with their old possessions and form one state." Then, breaking away from the memorized text, he added: "I repeat, one state, which we have seen in the cases of Normandy, Gascony, Burgundy, and Brittany—states that have long been united to the Kingdom of France."

Biagio said nothing. He lifted the manuscript from the desk, this time reading the next several passages to himself.

After a moment, he paraphrased: "You go on to say that men must either be caressed or annihilated." He set the manuscript down once again, an act that was beginning to look more like a nervous tic than a thoughtful pause. However, Biagio finally spoke his mind: "I take back any comments I might have made earlier that you will be criticized for your bold adherence to reality in this book," he stated in absolute seriousness. "Instead, judging from what I have read in just the first three chapters of a treatise that looks to be twenty-five chapters long, you will be rebuked, reviled, and excommunicated for it."

"Twenty-six," said Niccolò.

Biagio looked puzzled.

"Twenty-six chapters," clarified Niccolò. "I intend to compose a final exhortation soon, and if you read on, you will see that I provide support for my precepts with recent as well as ancient examples."

"There are those of us who know that you state simple reality, but why do you find it necessary to codify it in such a harsh manner?" said Biagio. "You will be vilified for it, mark my words."

"I have no doubt, but I am convinced that the principles I propose here are sound ones," countered Niccolò, "such as establishing colonies in rebel territories rather than leaving large garrisons to subdue the inhabitants."

Biagio tried to get a word in edgewise, but Niccolò carried on.

"A good leader should also make himself the defender of less powerful neighbors, and endeavor to weaken the stronger ones. For instance, the Romans always installed colonies in the provinces they acquired, always; and they made sure to entice the less powerful without increasing their strength; and perhaps most importantly, they did not allow foreign rulers to gain undue influence in their provinces. Never." Niccolò stood up from his chair to emphasize this last point. "The Romans behaved as all wise princes should; they considered not only present circumstances, but also guarded against future discords. The ability to see evils brewing in the distance makes them easier to remedy, and thus limits the likelihood of future wars."

"Most leaders do not possess the gift of divining future events," said Biagio. "Are you sure that you are not talking of an imaginary world as you accuse others of doing?" he added more as a provocation than an actual critique.

"Once again the Romans provide the path for us," said Niccolò. "Knowing that war could not be avoided, and that postponing it only gives advantage to the enemy, they declared war against Philip of Macedonia in Greece so as not to have to fight him on Italian soil."

Niccolò began pacing the room. He became more agitated; he started gesticulating wildly, and his voice rose several octaves.

"The French have ignored all these rules. Let us forget the disorder Charles left behind and concentrate on his cousin and successor, Louis XII. He ascended the throne in '98 only months before you and I began work at the Chancery, and he has made a shambles of our peninsula ever since. In a feeble attempt to avoid war, he ceded the territories closest to us in the Romagna to the Borgia pope, as well as virtually giving the Kingdom of Naples to Spain. He lost all of Lombardy because he did not adhere to any of the laws I stated here." Niccolò stopped his back and forth across the room, and turned his attention directly to Biagio. "If you will recall, I spoke of this matter with Cardinal Rohan in Nantes when Pope Alexander's son, Cesare Borgia, sat in the Romagna ready to strike us, and do you remember what the cardinal said?"

Biagio pointed to a phrase in the manuscript toward the end of the chapter. "You refer to his words right here: 'You Italians do not understand war.'" Biagio laughed as he thought back on that exchange between Niccolò and Cardinal Rohan. It had since become famous within the walls of the Palazzo Vecchio. "And then you replied—"

"'And you French do not understand politics!'" shouted Niccolò at the top of his lungs. "Because if they knew the slightest thing about it, they would never have allowed the Church to become so powerful."

Biagio read along as Niccolò recited, word for word, the next phrase he'd written: "History has shown us that France advanced the greatness of both Spain and the Church on our peninsula, and France's own ruin came precisely from the two of them. From which we can draw a general rule: Whoever is the cause of another becoming powerful is himself ruined."

"I could not agree more, my friend," said Biagio. "It was Pope Julius's sinister alliance with Ferdinand of Spain in the Holy League, along with the Republic of Venice, the duchy of Ferrara, Henry VIII of England, and the Emperor Maximilian, that sealed France's fate."

"And the fate of our free Republic," said Niccolò, his voice trembling with rage. "As France's sole ally on the peninsula, the vengeance of the pope and the Spanish armies on our dear city came swiftly."

Both Niccolò and Biagio remained silent as they relived the memories of those horrid days leading up to the fall of their beloved Republic only a short year ago.

"Keep reading," blurted Niccolò, snapping out of his reverie. "We've got a lot of work to do."

Chapter Thirteen

1499: THE LADY OF FORLÌ

Shortly after Niccolò was assigned the post at the Second Chancery, Marcello Adriano sent the neophyte secretary on his first diplomatic mission to Piombino, a port on the Tuscan coast, to speak with its ruler, Jacopo IV d'Appiano, who led an army on Florence's behalf in the war against Pisa. D'Appiano demanded a pay raise for himself equal to that of other prominent captains. In addition, he petitioned for an increase of troops. The rivalries between the various captains aiding the Florentine cause in Pisa gave rise to numerous complaints. Many demanded salary increases that not only encouraged an atmosphere of jealousy and infighting, but also naturally augmented the expenses of conducting an already costly war, which set off a series of problems for the city of Florence itself. As usual, the brunt of the financial burdens fell to the Florentine people, fomenting discontent and raising the threat of open rebellion. Niccolò made a name for himself on that mission by masterfully persuading d'Appiano to forgo an increase in salary in favor of a modest expansion of his military forces. With the war in Pisa a constant concern, Florence needed allied combatants to fall in line as d'Appiano did if victory was to be achieved. Unfortunately, other captains were not as accommodating.

Niccolò's success in Piombino made him and his negotiating expertise a valuable asset. A few months later, in midsummer, Chancellor Adriani handed him his first truly sensitive mission with a figure of notable import. Piombino had yielded to Florence's terms; now it was the city of Forlì's turn. Situated in Romagna, a region northeast of Florence, on the road to Ravenna, Forlì was home to Countess Caterina Sforza Riario, the illegitimate daughter of Galleazzo Maria Sforza, Duke of Milan, and niece to Ludovico il Moro. Noted for her extraordinary beauty and deep resolve, she had a violent past that succeeded in darkening her soul and inuring her feminine spirit. She governed her small, turbulent state from the time she was a young widow of twenty-six, when her first husband, Girolamo Riario, one of the original conspirators against the Pazzi, was murdered in his own palace in 1488, ironically the victim of a ruthless plot. In the aftermath of her husband's assassination by the rival Orsi family, Caterina and her children were taken as prisoners.

It didn't take long for Caterina's captors to realize that they needed to gain access to her castle in order to be safe from attack. Their numerous attempts to seize it were rebuffed by the castellan. To break the stalemate, Caterina assured the Orsi that if she were permitted to enter the castle she would relinquish it to them. In order to secure the deal, she agreed to leave her children with them as hostages. The moment she entered the castle walls, however, she climbed atop its ramparts and proceeded to rebuke her husband's killers, hurling insult upon insult, and threatening revenge. And as to the fate of her children, she lifted her gown and petticoat to reveal her genitals in a gesture of bold defiance, reminding her captors that she possessed the apparatus to generate as many children as she so desired. Her children's captors were so terrified by her actions that they dared not harm any of them. She later found the opportunity to take harsh and swift revenge against the Orsi family.

By the time Niccolò embarked on his two-day journey over the Apennines into Forlì, he'd heard Caterina's "genital" story from dozens of government officials in the Palazzo Vecchio. Biagio's version of the story was particularly spicy. Niccolò also heard about the countess's reprisal against the killers of her second husband, Giacomo Feo; renditions of that story were fewer and infinitely less colorful, but equally bloody. Feo was cut down while riding home with Caterina from a fox hunt. The countess lost no time galloping into Forlì to even the score. Forty people connected to the conspiracy died at the hands of Caterina's men, and as many as fifty were tortured and thrown into prison. Niccolò also knew full well that just a few months earlier, in the spring of 1499, Caterina's third husband, Giovanni de' Medici, known as "il Popolano," died in her arms of a serious illness.

All these stories, as tragic and brutal as they were, sifted through his mind as he reviewed the parameters of his mission. He knew he was up against a strong and determined ruler, a tough negotiator, and a hardened wife and mother. Getting ready for their meeting required meticulous preparation. The Signoria charged Niccolò with specific goals: They asked him to prevail upon Caterina's son, Ottaviano Riario, to fight in the war against Pisa without the salary hike he requested; they also wanted a procurement of as much gunpowder, saltpeter, and ammunition from the countess as possible.

Before leaving, Biagio begged Niccolò to bring home a

simple portrait of the notorious Lady of Forlì. Her female allure was legendary. In all probability Biagio was suffering deeply from the pangs of jealousy at his friend's good fortune to be in the presence of a woman whose acute mental capacity and physical qualities were capable of confounding and bewitching friends and foes alike. Biagio even went so far as to demand that Niccolò be careful to roll up the portrait gently. "Folding it would only ruin it," he said. "If she's half as beautiful as Botticelli painted her in his *Primavera,* I'm afraid you will never come home," he said, "and I will never get my portrait."

The first leg of the voyage westward over the Tuscan Apennines presented a considerable amount of danger due to the vertiginous slopes, which were, to a large degree, unstable and prone to landslides, including falling rocks, rivers of mud, and shifting masses of earth. Niccolò had strong equestrian skills, but never having made this particular journey, he paced himself carefully and stuck religiously to the well-beaten Tuscan-Romagna road, stopping to lodge quite early at an inn near San Benedetto in Alpe, deep in the wooded highlands. This section of the Apennines divided the peninsula between the Po Valley—a vast stretch of rich, flat land that hosted the Po river, Italy's largest waterway to the north—and the rolling hills of Latium and Tuscany to the south. Keeping transportation fluid and accessible over these slopes was essential to maintaining economic and political interaction. Although the ancient Romans depended on the Via Flaminia, a major thoroughfare between Rome and Romagna on the western coast, the direct route across the rugged terrain from Florence to Bologna, the largest city in Romagna, provided a considerably shorter and faster route under the proper conditions. Fortunately, the second half of the trip offered fewer dangers since the verdant foothills on the western slope, made up primarily of sedimentary rock, rolled gently toward the Adriatic Sea.

Niccolò arrived in the proximity of Rocca di Ravaldino, the site of Caterina's fortress on the southern outskirts of Forlì, late on the second day of his journey. The July heat had borne down on him throughout the entire trip, depleting his strength and acuity of mind, which only served to hasten his pace as he drew closer to his destination. He felt compelled to stop, however, to admire the fortress when he spotted it from a neighboring hillside. He took in its handsome design, seemingly impenetrable walls fortified by buttresses surrounding the entire structure, and stout circular towers jutting out at its corners. Being a relatively new structure, the stone maintained its original umber hue, making its grandeur all the more imposing against the summer sky and endless turquoise sea in the distance.

The drawbridge lowered the moment Niccolò arrived at the main gate. He watched as scores of soldiers appeared on the ramparts and filled each arrow loop. When the massive wooden plank finally locked into place, Niccolò ambled slowly and deliberately through the heavily manned gatehouse and strode into the courtyard, where he was met by an agent of the countess and a squad of four armed soldiers who escorted him directly to his quarters. Once settled in, Niccolò washed up and rested for an hour or so to recuperate from the long day's journey. His room provided him with all the amenities and luxuries afforded a foreign dignitary. He stood at the room's only window, laced with heavy wrought iron bars, and looked out onto a vast meadow hemmed in by a dense forest that seemed to go on forever. A faint scent of salty air wafted in from the east. For that brief moment he thanked his lucky stars to be far from the mosquito-infested Arno valley.

A knock at his door woke him from his reverie. A young page entered with the news that the countess had retired to her chambers and that she would very much like to make Niccolò's acquaintance first thing in the morning. As Niccolò had missed dinner due to his late arrival, a second page entered a few minutes later with a hefty portion of *gran bollito misto,* a hearty stew made with seven different cuts of boiled beef and veal, and seven more supplementary varieties of meat including capon, broiler chicken, and beef tongue. A condiment reduced from a base of cooked carrots, parsley, boiled eggs, olive oil, and vinegar accompanied the bollito, as did a basket of freshly baked *piadine,* the typical flat bread of the region. Niccolò lost no time digging into his meal, which he washed down with several glasses of Sangiovese, the local red wine. He slept like a baby that night.

The following morning after a light breakfast of sweet wine, fresh figs wrapped in razor-thin slices of prosciutto, and *tigelle,* a slightly thicker version of the flat bread he had the previous evening, Niccolò was accompanied by the same young page to the countess's office, a simple room connected to her bedchambers. He sat at a long, rustic chestnut table, alone, surrounded by a dozen unassuming straight-backed chairs. The dark stone walls had every bit the feeling of a military camp. No artwork embellished the entire space, and nothing other than the chestnut table graced the rough, unpolished granite floor. Despite the blistering heat of July, a damp but welcomed chill hung in the air. After a while, the page showed his face again with a plate of almond biscuits. He set them on the table without saying a word and promptly walked off. While he waited, Niccolò bided his time reviewing his notes and nibbling on one biscuit after another, which he found to be similar to and just as addictive as the *cantucci di Prato* his mother baked when he was a child.

At last, the double doors to the countess's chamber opened. Niccolò immediately stood up and approached the door in readiness for Caterina's entrance. The first person to walk in, however, was not the countess but a tall, well-built young man. He wore his chin high, and failed to look Niccolò in the eye as he strode in. His gentle aspect commanded respect, which Niccolò paid him with a slight nod and an even slighter bend of the knee. He introduced himself as a representative of the Sforza family in Milan, which Niccolò interpreted as a reminder to him, and to Florence, that the countess enjoyed a close connection and military alliance with her uncle, Duke Ludovico il Moro.

"The countess begs your pardon. She will join us shortly," said the man as he took a seat at the table. "She is caring for her youngest child. He has fallen quite ill."

After everything Niccolò had heard about Caterina's qualities of "manly" intellect, courage, and the deep respect her troops had for her, not to mention the infamous story of her abandoning her children to their abductors, he was naturally taken aback, and frankly quite impressed, to hear of such concern for her young child. Usually these matters were left to nursemaids or assistants in noble households such as these, but clearly Caterina Sforza did not follow expected rules or norms.

"It is my honor to be here," responded Niccolò to the representative from Milan. "A leader must tend to all his, or her, duties, big or small." He sat down across from the representative and waited.

An hour and several more biscuits later, Caterina burst

into the room unannounced. Both men jumped to their feet at her presence. This first glance of the countess made a lasting impression on Niccolò. The women of Florence enjoyed a much deserved reputation of sophistication, elegance, and physical appeal, but Caterina added a look of moral dignity and confidence to those qualities that made her rise above the rest. There was no denying her allure. Her thick auburn hair, pulled back and braided to expose a strong and noble forehead, produced a distinct look of respectability. The tufts of meticulously twined hair coiled over her ears gave the appearance of two stylish, and intentionally mischievous, horns on either side of her head. Pearls and semi-precious stones laced a silk hairnet holding it all neatly in place.

"My apologies," she said, taking a seat at her representative's side and directly across from Niccolò.

"It is my pleasure, Madam Countess Caterina Sforza," said Niccolò with a differential nod of the head.

After several minutes of small talk and general niceties, Niccolò felt it was time to dive into the heart of the matter.

"We would want very much for Ottaviano to continue his command against our enemies in Pisa," he said.

"I am not surprised," the countess responded. "His skills as captain of his troops have undoubtedly saved Florentine lives and money."

Her eyes held Niccolò's gaze, never wavering for a second. Niccolò saw pure strength and determination in those eyes. She, too, wore her chin high, a Sforza family trait, perhaps, and her lips creased ever so slightly in a smirk—or was it simply a show of anger?

Niccolò could not tell. He eventually perceived it to be

impatience. *But impatience about what?* he asked himself. He concluded that she didn't want to beat around the bush, and wasn't the least bit interested in the obligatory round of compliments and flattery that usually preceded requests for money or favors. Confident that he'd divined her state of mind accurately, Niccolò skipped right to the point.

"We value your friendship highly," he said, "but the Republic of Florence regrets it cannot meet your demands for an increase in salary."

"My son asks only what so many others have asked," replied the countess.

"There will be no increase in the salary for any captain that is allied to our cause," said Niccolò, noticing the smirk on her face twist slightly into a smile, which he found perplexing. He plowed forward. "It is not our intention to dishonor you, Madam Countess, or discredit the service of your son."

"I am not asking you to raise the salaries of the other captains in your service," said the countess, "only the salary of Forlì's captain, Ottaviano Riario, lord of Imola and Forlì."

"I have not come prepared to grant any increases, my lady," said Niccolò.

"Then I'm afraid you have wasted your time coming all this way," she said, leaning into him as if to proffer a free piece of advice.

"I believe my coming here is to our mutual benefit," replied Niccolò, still trying to decipher the meaning behind her sudden smile.

"If Florence refuses to honor our request, then, forgive me, where is the benefit for us?" she asked flatly.

"We can pay handsomely for weapons and equipment,

however, should you care to enter into a discussion for them," said Niccolò. "We are prepared to purchase substantial quantities of saltpeter and gunpowder as well."

"You proffer money for what I do not have, and none at all for what I do have," she said. "My uncle in Milan has made me a more reasonable offer."

Now that she had brought up Ludovico il Moro, Niccolò saw no reason to circumvent the subject of King Louis XII's imminent attack on the duchy of Milan, and her uncle's almost certain defeat. Although this visit to Forlì marked the first real diplomatic mission of strategic importance for him, and his female opponent possessed the backbone of a warrior, the acumen of a scholar, and the cunning of a thief, Niccolò felt well at ease and quite comfortable to lay his cards on the table.

"Milan finds itself on the wrong side against the Kingdom of France, which would leave Forlì defenseless to the north, while Cesare Borgia, and the Borgia pope's plans to acquire Romagna, squeeze you from the south," he said.

"Valentino, as Cesare so desires to be called, and his bold advances into our territory threaten the Florentine Republic as well," the countess replied.

"And that is where we must come together," said Niccolò.

"I shall deal with Valentino when the time comes," she said without blinking an eye.

"At which time, I trust, you will call upon Florence for her help, which we are prepared to offer."

The countess shifted in her seat. "Florence has often uttered words of support, but I have yet to be convinced by her deeds," she countered.

"What has Forlì to offer in exchange for our protection?" said Niccolò abruptly.

"Have you forgotten our aid to your cause against the Venetians in the Casentino?" she said, her voice flavored with indignation.

Realizing that the countess's honor had been ruffled, Niccolò pivoted to a softer tone. "I repeat, the Republic of Florence values your friendship."

For a split second she locked eyes with the representative from Milan. Although he betrayed no reaction one way or another, the countess turned to Niccolò and replied without hesitation: "You need more men in your fight against the Pisans, and we can give you those men."

Niccolò paused a moment to consider her last words. For her part, the countess never divulged a hint of apprehension or uncertainty. Despite the stifling heat, she remained calm and collected, almost bored by it all. Her eyes stayed fixed on Niccolò, who, for his part, felt right at home in such a combative environment.

"I will pose your offer to our Signoria," he finally replied.

The meeting drew to a close soon after those remarks. The countess retired to her chamber accompanied by her representative, and Niccolò returned immediately to his quarters to compose a letter to the Signoria on the day's events. He knew that in order to come away from this mission with any semblance of success, her request for an increase in salary for her son would have to be addressed. It was simply a question of honor, which was not some lofty ideal, but a crucial and practical consideration. Caterina was a proud woman who spoke as much in the name of her family's honor as she did for the welfare of Forlì and its people. Under no circumstance could she allow herself to be perceived by her beloved uncle in Milan to be buckling under Florentine pressure.

Niccolò spent the rest of the morning writing his report to the Signoria and mailed it out that very afternoon. He enjoyed a good part of the remainder of day playing cards with an assortment of squires, pages, and attendants, all of whom seemed to have plenty of time on their hands. In the evening, just prior to dinner, he sat with a band of spirited young courtiers as they practiced lines of a farcical play, the *Menaechmi,* by the Roman playwright Plautus. The manuscript, which was making the rounds of the Italian courts, had recently been rediscovered in its original Latin form after being lost or neglected for over a millennium. Its transliteration into the local idiom gave it a distinctly modern feel, and the excitement over it was palpable. Florence dabbled in the translation and reinvention of classic Roman plays as part of its humanistic tradition, but not to the extent of the northern courts like Ferrara and Urbino. Niccolò watched in fascination as the actors ran through a plot loaded with mistaken identities, sheer nonsense, and a complex series of comedic mishaps and errors. He quickly found a chair and sat down, convinced there was no other place he'd rather be. *What a refreshing change from the same old sacred representations of Our Lord's life and death,* he thought to himself.

Florence's confraternities and other religious groups recreated iconic scenes from the life of Jesus Christ with great emotion and often with sophisticated theatrics during Christmas and Easter, but Niccolò always felt more drawn to the feast of Carnival, where all that is blessed and sacrosanct is turned on its head, giving way to mischief and transgression. The stock characters he saw in this play, all derived from ancient Roman stereotypes—like the mischievous servant, comic courtesan, doddering old man, blustering academic, and shrewd ruffian—still rang true. The wit and intelligence of it all, despite its apparent silliness, profoundly impressed Niccolò, who was viewing this style of performance with virgin eyes. He recognized instantly how the structure of this particular theatrical form, the earthiness of its characters, the freedom of movement, and the sheer entertainment value made for an excellent tool of communication. *Hearing wisdom from the mouths of servants and seeing buffoonery in the actions of nobles or lust in the hearts of the clergy is the world as it really is,* he mused.

As the summer sun descended behind the Apennine foothills, dozens of members of the countess's inner circle of bureaucrats, courtiers, and family members began to assemble for dinner in the grand hall. Caterina took her place at the main table next to the representative from Milan. Niccolò sat to her left as her guest of honor. A host of confidants and high-ranking officers of the court filled out the rest of the table. The countess's demeanor seemed relaxed and natural, betraying no hint of her sentiments regarding the morning's discussions. Niccolò, too, found himself quite comfortable, and felt no particular inclination to engage in any line of inquiry or discussion even remotely having to do with the French, Pope Alexander VI, the war in Pisa, or politics in general. All he could talk about was the hysterically funny play he had seen rehearsed earlier that evening. Everyone joined in on the discussion with tales of performances they had witnessed in the court of Ferrara.

"A young poet by the name of Ludovico Ariosto is already experimenting with writing original plays in the ancient style," said one of the courtiers.

The representative from Milan, who hadn't spoken more than five words all day, perked up. "He steals everything he knows from a young man who hails from your territories," he said, addressing his remarks to Niccolò. "He goes by the name of Bibbiena, after the town of his birth in the Casentino. The man is brilliant."

"I have never heard of him," replied Niccolò.

"You will. He was a friend of the Medici before their fall," said the representative, "and has been a guest of Guidobaldo da Montefeltro and Elisabetta Gonzaga in Urbino ever since."

"Both Ariosto and Bibbiena owe much to the plays of Publius Terentius Afer as well—or Terence, as we call him," said a wizened confidant at the end of the table.

"And Giovanni Boccaccio," added another, whom Niccolò recognized as one of the actors from earlier. "The backbone of their original comedies is that of the ancient Romans and Greeks, but in their heart these plays speak of people today."

In all the years that Niccolò frequented the libraries, lecture halls, and street corners of Florence, he had never been so intimately exposed to the world of theater. It was truly a strange, new experience for him. To some extent, sacred representations and mystery plays satisfied all the theatrical curiosity of the Florentines. Not to say that his native city lacked the culture to embrace it—far from it—but theater as a performing art flourished primarily in the courts, where considerable numbers of cultured men and women were sequestered in castles, palazzos, and even military fortresses far from the diversions of a lively community. They had to provide their own entertainment, often on a nightly basis, or die of boredom. Besides being an open, vibrant city, Florence produced humanistic efforts focused primarily on uncovering the truth behind the history of the ancient world, its political oratories, and philosophy. And, of course, the city led the western world in the visual arts such as painting and sculpture, as well as in the literary fields of poetry, prose, and theater as a form of literature.

As the local gastronomic delicacies continued to be brought to the table and the Sangiovese flowed freely, the conversation grew increasingly more engaging. Niccolò quickly realized that he'd found a new avocation of sorts. His attraction to this art form ran too deep to be ignored. Caterina, too, participated openly in the discussions throughout the evening. Her rapport with the members of her court seemed to flow without pretense or artificiality. The bond she had created with them felt more like camaraderie among soldiers than a hierarchy of aristocrats. She laughed wholeheartedly and without hesitation along with everyone around the table, all of them strong-willed and assertive men, as they recounted their salacious exploits with renowned courtesans. She always spoke with feminine elegance and grace, however, while her voice resounded with authority and conviction. The respect she garnered from all of those around her was evident. Something about her demanded it. During those stolen moments when Niccolò could observe her without being noticed, he studied her bearing and her manner, and marveled at her ability to disarm you as much as empower you with a simple glance.

After dinner, Niccolò walked the dark halls of the fortress toward his bedchambers replaying the events of the day in his head. His meeting with the countess that morning ended with what seemed to be a mutually acceptable deal in place. He was quite pleased with himself for holding firm on her request for more money for her son, while agreeing that she would provide more soldiers for the conflict in Pisa in exchange for Florence's promise of protection. Most importantly, the friendship between the two states remained robust and secure. In reality, this was the Signoria's ultimate goal. The security of the Republic was at stake. Both Niccolò and the countess possessed the political acumen to realize that France's blatant support of Alexander VI's expansionistic policies posed an existential threat to both their states.

Along with Niccolò's sense of accomplishment, however, came a recognition, an epiphany of sorts, of a deep-seated yearning to express himself more openly and freely. He realized that his view of the world, his thoughts and convictions, could now be channeled through a new art form that had taken its cue from the ancient Romans and Greeks. The possibilities seemed endless. Above all, as he lay in bed pondering the day and preparing for his next formal meeting with the countess in the days to come, he came to grips with the fact that he had found a respectable outlet for his devilish wit and natural penchant for satire.

Several days passed without word from anyone in the Signoria. Two missives finally arrived on the fifth day, one from Biagio and the other from the Council of the Ten of War. Biagio, of course, wrote to inquire about the portrait he'd requested. He also implored Niccolò to hurry home as soon as possible. The workload had piled up, and the Second Chancery found itself in complete chaos due to Niccolò's absence. It seemed that the ruthlessness and brutality of the political world didn't hold a candle to the damage caused by the innuendo and gossip of day-to-day office politics. Envy, jealously, competitiveness, and vitriol ran rampant. Now that their boss was away on a mission, the entire staff of the Second Chancery reported directly to the chancellor on all issues great and small. But Adriani's upper-crust demeanor and formality did little to quell the discord. In fact, it festered. According to Biagio, the only one who could remedy the situation was "il Machia." Niccolò wasn't sure exactly why, but these words from Biagio threw him into a fit of laughter.

Conversely, the news from the Ten of War dampened Niccolò's spirits considerably. They stressed that under no circumstances should he agree to raise Ottaviano's salary. In fact, they held the line on all things regarding their purse strings. Florence's continued friendship with the countess remained the centerpiece of their concerns. Regardless of being given absolutely no room to bargain further, Niccolò remained confident that the verbal accord he had made with the countess would hold.

There was one piece of information from the Signoria that pleased him greatly, however. His immediate superiors commended him on his progress and paid him special tribute for the quality and style of his correspondence, which not only described the objective realities on the ground, but also reached into the hearts and minds of the other negotiators and grasped their very thoughts and feelings. The senior officials in Florence realized they were no longer receiving simple records of events, but rather valuable intelligence. Of course, the Signoria did not spell out their praise in so many words; they merely gave him a perfunctory pat on the back. No need to have this go to his head, they inevitably thought. Niccolò, however, quite able to read between the lines, immediately picked up on the level of appreciation they had for his work. *Once I bring home a signed agreement by the Countess of Forlì,* he thought, *my success will be complete.*

The meeting set for the morning of the sixth day was scheduled to be the last between the two states. Niccolò had drawn up an agreement that simply required the countess's signature. This would occupy a minor portion of the day's activities, and he would be on his way back to Florence immediately after that. Caterina made her entrance into the chamber in fine form, as always. As had become ritual, Ludovico il Moro's representative from Milan stood at her side. And as usual, he spoke only when spoken to. Niccolò assumed that the representative had communicated daily with Milan just as he had done with the Signoria. The Sforzas were a tight-knit clan and information between members of the family traveled at lightning speed. Given the threats of war from France, taking particular aim at the duchy of Milan, il Moro's interest in Florence's maneuvers must have been extremely high. Caterina had, no doubt, received missives over the past several days from her uncle with suggestions or counteroffers, but her facial expression and body language hinted at nothing, at least nothing out of the ordinary. By all indications, everything seemed to be right on track.

The three of them took the same seats as on their first meeting. Niccolò leaned forward in his straight-backed chair to slide the parchment stating the terms of their agreement across the table. The representative intercepted it and placed it neatly in front of Caterina. Niccolò noticed immediately that he had neglected to slide the plume and inkwell over to her as well. The countess's eyes only briefly glanced down at the parchment. Her main focus remained on Niccolò.

"I take it there is nothing written here regarding an increase in salary for my Ottaviano?" she asked.

Niccolò did all he could to hide his dismay. *We have already done away with this question,* he thought to himself. He affected a smile.

"Florence's promise to come to the defense of your sovereign state in exchange for more troops in Pisa are the terms on which we had agreed, my Lady," he said, letting the smile slip away to underscore his concern.

Niccolò suspected from the start that the issue of salary was not really about money, or even about her son. He wrote to the Signoria about the countess's strong sense of honor. He told them in no uncertain terms that everything revolved around that one virtue. He begged them to show more liberality and pay the countess the respect she deserved. He carefully described all of this to his superiors in the Signoria not because he thought the bargain they had orally agreed on was in jeopardy, although having an extra bargaining chip never hurt, but because the constant presence of Ludovico il Moro's representative in Caterina's court worried him. The Duke of Milan had established quite a name for himself as a ruthless, untrustworthy, double-dealing, and opportunistic ruler during France's first incursion into the peninsula, and Niccolò knew that a leopard did not change his spots. *Had Milan made the countess a better offer?* he wondered.

"In fairness, I only ask that his salary match that of other captains of equal rank and stature," the countess said.

"With all due respect, my Lady, I thought I had made the position of our government clear from the onset regarding the issue of Ottaviano's salary," said Niccolò.

"Then your answer is still no?" she asked flatly.

"I daresay you are being shortsighted," he responded. "Surely you can see that maintaining our friendship as well as securing Florence's protection from the dangers to your sovereignty posed by Cesare Borgia from the south, and the French threat to your family and allies in the north, far outweigh any temporary, monetary benefit we, or anyone, can offer you."

"I trust the friendship between our two states is not in question," she demurred.

That's when Niccolò realized he had been outsmarted. The countess knew all along that Florence sought nothing more out of these negotiations than good relations with her neighbors.

"Your friendship is of vital importance to us," Niccolò reiterated, "as ours must be to you, my Lady."

And with that, Countess Caterina, the Lady of Forlì, smiled warmly at Niccolò and rose from the table. In deference to her, Niccolò was quick to rise as well.

She said nothing at first; her countenance remained affable and unassuming, and finally she whispered in an almost motherly tone: "Then friends we shall remain." She nodded respectfully, begged forgiveness for having to leave so abruptly, and marched out of the room.

Niccolò watched her leave, dumbfounded. He picked up the unsigned agreement from the table and left. Within an hour's time he had saddled his horse and was on his way.

As Niccolò journeyed home over the soft eastern slopes of the Apennines and down the tortuous paths into the Casentino, his thoughts kept returning to the week's encounter. He could see clearly how imprudent and reckless the whole endeavor had been.

Caterina would be left without a true friend to protect her when Cesare Borgia storms into her territory with the aid of French troops as he inevitably will, he mused. *Florence would find itself with a lethal enemy knocking at its eastern door, and Italy would continue to bend to the will of foreign powers.*

Chapter Fourteen

1513: "ONE'S OWN ARMS AND ABILITY"

The night of reading, analyzing, and positing comments and suggestions on Niccolò's little book passed without major incident. Reviewing Niccolò's words and ideas with the author standing right next to him tested Biagio's stamina. He read carefully and attentively through all of its twenty-five chapters before calling it quits.

The next morning, after a sparse breakfast of diluted red wine and a few slices of stale bread, Niccolò hurried outside into the damp, wintry air to tend to his usual duties. Biagio stayed inside with Marietta. The Christmas season was approaching, which meant lots of baking, especially her famous *panforte*, a sort of candied cake crammed full of nuts, dried fruits, spices, and honey. Her particular version of this holiday dessert included a good portion of white grapes that hung to dry in their wine cellar for this year's Vin Santo.

Biagio, one of the few males in his social rung who actually ventured into a kitchen, graciously offered to lend a hand.

Marietta, of course, didn't need his help. The wives and daughters of the hired woodcutters and groundskeepers performed most of the womanly chores in that part of the house. But she enjoyed his company, and used the opportunity to catch up on the latest gossip coming out of Florence. She hadn't been back there since their departure nine months earlier. For his part, Biagio couldn't bear for someone to bake a sweet Christmas bread without him nibbling on all the spare walnuts and candied orange rinds left on the cutting board. He willingly provided all the gossip she wanted.

When Niccolò returned from his morning's activities, he immediately summoned Biagio to join him at the inn across the way. It was where he preferred having his second, and more substantial, breakfast of cured meats and cheese. A short glass of red wine was also in order on such a cold day. And besides, he had a lot he urgently wanted to discuss.

Biagio wandered in and sat across from Niccolò in a far corner of the inn's communal area, a good distance from much of the commotion. Gianluca, the innkeeper, brought over a hefty plate of *finocchiona*, a fennel-cured salami; several fresh cuts of *casciotta* cheese; and a tin of generously salted *schiacciata*, the local focaccia bread. Having worked up quite an appetite, Niccolò started eating the moment the plate hit the table. Biagio hesitated, which caught Niccolò's immediate attention.

"Are you ill?" asked Niccolò, genuinely concerned.

"The country air couldn't be better for me," said Biagio. "I feel great."

Niccolò laughed out loud. "How could I be so stupid?" he said. "My workers told me they brought a sack of walnuts to the kitchen just this morning. Marietta must be making her *panforte*."

Biagio wiped the guilty grin from his face and tore himself a slab of schiacciata. "Isn't there something more important you'd rather talk about?" he said sheepishly.

"Of course there is," said Niccolò. "You looked puzzled during many parts of your reading last night. That worried me."

Biagio sat up in his chair; his eyes opened wide as if he'd just woken up. He didn't expect to dive right into a discussion on *The Prince* so soon. He pondered what Niccolò had just said.

"I was not puzzled at all, Machia . . . well, perhaps a little, but your words are clear, and dare I say direct and quite simple, but so loaded with meaning. It is difficult to read what you have written without pausing to contemplate their truths."

Niccolò remained silent, waiting for Biagio to explain himself.

Biagio finally added: "They penetrate our commonplace beliefs, the truths we hold dear, and they reveal uncomfortable, but even deeper, truths."

"People are people, my friend," said Niccolò, "nothing more."

Biagio wasn't quite sure what he meant, but continued on: "Your Moses, for example, is a conqueror, a prince, and not a prophet as the Church teaches us. Can you blame me if I seemed puzzled?"

"If one is to judge by his deeds, then Moses differs little from great men such as Cyrus, King of Persia, or Romulus or Theseus," said Niccolò in a sober tone. "And what makes him as worthy as these other great kings of history is that he owes everything to Virtue, and nothing to Fortune. He took the opportunities presented before him and shaped them to his needs. He was a prophet who founded a kingdom, and should be deemed worthy of our admiration."

"Unlike Savonarola," mused Biagio.

"As you read in my little book last evening, there is nothing more difficult to carry out, nor more doubtful of success, nor more dangerous to manage, than to initiate a new order of things," said Niccolò. "Like those other kings, the prophet Moses, despite being a man of God, could never have created a homeland and maintained its constitution without the use of arms. You know that as well as I do."

"It is fair to say, then, that Julius II, the warrior pope, had learned much from Moses," said Biagio.

"As did his predecessor," added Niccolò.

"Alexander VI himself was not a warrior, however. He had his son, Cesare, do his bidding."

"Quite true. Whatever can be said of Ludovico il Moro's duplicity can be applied tenfold to the Borgia pope. The Church grew much richer and more prosperous under his command."

Gianluca finally brought a short carafe of wine, poured them each a healthy cupful, and hurried off. The wine helped the discussion along, which soon digressed into the pros and cons of Pope Alexander VI's reign, going all the way back to his election in '92. Taking full advantage of his family's tremendous wealth, extravagant promises, and heavy doses of intimidation, Rodrigo Borgia of Valencia, Spain, had extorted votes that were originally intended for other candidates to secure the papacy. His propensity for corruption and intrigue went completely unchecked. In fact, the other cardinals in the conclave gladly sold their influence and their dignity to the highest bidder. They demonstrated no regard for ethics, morals, or the fate of their very souls.

Pope Alexander VI was so dominant a personage in Italian history that both Niccolò and Biagio couldn't talk about important events of the period without continually bringing up his name. They compared Alexander to previous popes who had led unseemly lives, often given to extravagance and vice. But he was the first to display such unabashed vulgarity and debauchery while holding the office, they both agreed, to say nothing of the acts of murder and intrigue committed by him or in his name.

Whereas previous popes were more discreet, Alexander made no mystery of having sired numerous offspring. In fact, he was a proud and jealous father who would do anything for his children in hopes of expanding his own personal power and territory. He loved them with such passion that enhancing their wealth and position became the driving force behind his crimes, all of which were carried out with cold detachment, and no inkling of remorse or scruple. He oldest son, Giovanni, became the Duke of Gandia; his infamous daughter, Lucrezia, married into three influential families, each ending in either scandal or tragic death; Goffredo, the youngest son, was also used by his father to secure the family's power through numerous marriages; and most importantly, Cesare, also known as the Duke of Valentino, whom Niccolò had met several times, set out to annex much of Romagna to the Papal State as part of his father's expansionistic policies.

"I was not surprised that there is so much concerning Cesare Borgia in your little book," said Biagio.

"I trust, then, that you agree when I say that if one considers his character and his conduct, there exists no better example of how a new prince must act."

"Once again, however, do you not think words such as 'a prince must be both beast and man,' despite being sadly true, will irritate the eyes of those who read them, and be impossible to pronounce for cultured men such as the Medici? Lorenzo is your intended reader, is he not?"

"The ancient Greeks and Romans taught their princes to summon their animal nature as well, but they disguised it behind metaphor and myth," said Niccolò. "Was not Achilles, the ancient world's greatest warrior, educated by the centaur, Chiron, half beast and half man?"

"Whatever can be said of you, Machia, you are not one to disguise your teachings," said Biagio with a smile.

"If men were all good, this precept of using our animal nature would not be necessary, but as we all know, this is not the case," replied Niccolò.

He knew Biagio was only playing devil's advocate, but having to defend his ideas, as he'd had to do countless times while working in the Chancery, wore him down. His letters to the Signoria nearly always recounted the political situation in stark terms and as it truly presented itself, with his comments and suggestions slipped in along the way, but more often than not, his recommendations were bypassed in the name of expediency and convenience. In truth, it often took too much political courage to follow his lead.

"I write what I see," he added by way of self-defense.

Biagio reached down and picked up a slice of finocchiona and folded it into his mouth. He washed it down with a slug of wine. "Let me see . . ." he said, trying to recall a line from last night's reading, "ah, yes, a prince must be both like a lion and a fox?"

"For a lion can too easily be trapped, and a fox is no match for the power of a wolf," replied Niccolò. "Cesare Borgia perfectly embodies that nature."

"You pronounced those exact words ten years ago when you returned from your first visit with Cesare Borgia," said Biagio. "I remember it as clear as day."

The mention of that period in his life gave Niccolò a moment's pause. Much had happened since he'd been given his position at the Chancery. His father, Bernardo, had recently died, and shortly after that, he married Marietta. He was also relatively new at his job and still had much to learn. His meetings with the Lady of Forlì and with the various unscrupulous *condottieri* fighting throughout Italy taught him much about the cold, dispassionate world of Italian politics, and his visit to the French court to settle issues regarding the Pisan war opened his eyes to the vulnerability of the Florentine Republic and the entire peninsula. The sense of rebellion that grew in his heart against these foreign aggressors during those years never faded. The unique perspective he enjoyed as Florence's chief ambassador shined a light on that aggression, and the love he harbored for his homeland put it all into intense focus. When he eventually met the young, ruthless, and cunning Cesare Borgia in Urbino, he knew he had found a suitable model for the man who could save Italy from itself. A redeemer of sorts. Niccolò was wise enough, and savvy enough in the ways of the world, to know that Italy must first be ripped from the jaws of its predators beyond the Alps like France, Spain, and the Holy Roman Empire, using all means necessary, before it could ever pretend to find true freedom.

When Niccolò journeyed to Urbino in 1502 with Francesco Soderini, bishop of Volterra, to meet Cesare Borgia, the young duke had already done away with many of Romagna's petty despots by means of deception and sheer brutality. Soderini described the twenty-seven-year-old *condottiere* in his report to the Signoria as a forceful man in military matters who finds no enterprise too daunting, and never stops seeking glory and the enlargement of his state; a man who fears no enterprise, nor is he ever deterred by any dangers in his path.

"My letter to the Signoria told of a crafty young man, mysterious and mercurial in his actions, with Fortune seemingly always on his side," said Niccolò, staring into space as he recalled his first meeting with Cesare Borgia nearly twelve years ago. "It was a scorching hot summer afternoon," he mused. "I remember it as if it were yesterday . . . ."

Francesco Soderini and Niccolò sat patiently at the rectangular trestle table in Cesare Borgia's office in Urbino's Palazzo Ducale. The two massive windows situated directly behind them revealed miles of densely forested foothills to the southwest. Sunlight flooded in, washing over everyone and everything in the room. Soderini's sixty-year-old frame still held its dignified and noble stature, and his eyes, although dimming with age, gleamed with the intensity of his youth. He had retired from his duties as bishop during the previous year, and was living out the rest of his life as counselor and advisor to the Republic. His wisdom and experience complemented Niccolò's raw natural instincts. The two Florentine emissaries situated themselves directly across from Cesare Borgia, who had entered the room alone and took a seat without fanfare or flourish. Long coal-black hair accentuated his ashen complexion and tight, determined jawline. His face could be described as nothing short of solemn. Niccolò quickly identified his most elusive and menacing feature, the one aspect that made it virtually impossible to read his thoughts or discern his intentions: his penetrating and inscrutable gaze. It bore right through you.

Cesare had made a name for himself in the past year by sweeping across the Romagna, devouring any and all territory in his path. He'd already earned the titles of Duke of Valentino and

Urbino, Prince of Andria, gonfalonier and captain-general of the Church, and Lord of Piombino—and was well on his way to adding Imola, Faenza, Caterina's city of Forlì, and perhaps even the Republic of Florence to his list of conquests. The two Florentine emissaries came to the recently captured city of Urbino knowing full well that the Duke of Valentino, the title by which they addressed him, planned his next major act of aggression against Bologna, an important hub for culture and commerce, presently under the jurisdiction of Giovanni Bentivoglio. As they walked into the meeting, they were also quite aware of the fact that Louis XII of France, who protected the duke's adventures into the Romagna, had put the brakes on his military exploits, fearing they would irreparably upset the region's political balance. At the same time, several of the duke's principal captains, petty tyrants one and all, were beginning to plot against him in an effort to thwart any potential advancement of his troops into their personal strongholds. Being the senior emissary, Soderini instructed Niccolò to allow the duke to be the first to speak.

"I wish to be friends," said the duke straight off, "but allow me to be clear. Your Republic borders on a good portion of my territories, and I wish to be absolutely certain that I have nothing to fear from you."

Soderini waited to make sure the duke had completed his thought before replying. "I can assure you that our Republic seeks friendship and nothing more," he said.

Niccolò tried his hardest to decipher what the slight upward curl of the duke's lips signified. Was it the start of a warm, appreciative smile or was he simply holding back a smirk? In any event, Niccolò decided to follow up on Soderini's overture.

"Our Republic has no intention of aiding the conspirators against you," Niccolò said.

The duke burst out laughing. "Very good! You know of my situation. Bravo!" he said. "But make no mistake, I am ready to use the entirety of my strength against you should I feel you wish to do me harm." Then, before Soderini could respond to his threat, the duke continued: "Last year I could have imposed my harsh rule upon your Republic. I could have humiliated you, but I chose not to do so. Now listen carefully, and heed what I have to say: I do not in the least approve of this republican government of yours. I simply do not trust it. So if you do not want me as a friend, then you will see what it is like to have me as an enemy."

Niccolò's blood boiled. The duke's condemnation of Florence's Republic injured him like a stake through the heart. His mind raced with countless reasons why Florence's free Republic stood above all other forms of government, but his eyes revealed none of it. They remained focused on the duke, neither too steely and unbending in their regard of him nor too submissive or agreeable.

"I can assure you that if we are happy with the Republic as it stands," Niccolò said, indicating Soderini and himself, "then everyone is happy with it."

"We have not come all this way to insult anyone, nor to be insulted," growled Soderini, doing nothing to disguise his distaste for the duke's brashness.

Once again, the duke could not contain his laughter. It seemed to percolate up from the bottom of his gut. He couldn't have been having a better time! Niccolò, a man still unversed in the practical affairs of state, and who tended toward careful scrutiny rather than immediate action, now had a cocky young fighter before him, a man who had more in common with a brigand than a statesman. However, he also saw a man who possessed the mental, emotional, and physical tools to mold a state out of nothing. No easy task. Aided by his inexhaustible temerity and craftiness, he overran his enemies one by one, and it was precisely these two qualities that impressed Niccolò and summoned up so much of his admiration for him.

The duke ended his laughter as abruptly as it started, and turned his heartless stare to Soderini. "I must tell you that I had no hand in the Orsini plans to attack your Republic, nor in Vitellozzo Vitelli's adventures in Arezzo—although, I must say, I do not regret it," he said in a steady, sober voice. "I hope you did not come here thinking that I would somehow justify my actions with you, or those of my captains, for that matter."

Soderini took a deep breath. He wanted desperately to move away from this back-and-forth of threats and vicious barbs, but could not let the duke's words stand. It was time to start playing some of the diplomatic cards he had in his deck.

"You must certainly be aware of the treaty we have signed with the French king," Soderini said. "He has promised to protect our city and territories from attack."

The duke seemed unfazed. "I have much more insight into the king's intentions than you," he said flatly. "If you trust him, you are bigger fools than I imagined." He paused to study their reaction. Soderini's anger continued to escalate, and Niccolò, of course, maintained his composure.

The duke went on: "I would have to be a fool to speak to you in this manner if I did not already have the French behind me, no matter what they say to you or what you may have signed." He rose from his seat and peered down at them with looks that alternated between menacing and amicable. "Let me ask you, then: Why would you put your trust in someone so far away when you have the offer of friendship right here?"

Without uttering another word, or even bidding farewell, he turned and marched out of the room.

Seeing that Niccolò's mind had drifted a thousand miles away, Biagio scooped up the last remaining slab of casciotta. His appetite had returned with a vengeance as he sat there watching Niccolò eat. Niccolò, who never missed a trick, reached over and grabbed Biagio's hand before he could bite into it.

"I wanted you to know that I have instructed Gianluca to strap you with the bill," said Niccolò.

"That goes without saying, Machia my friend. After all, I am a guest in your house," said Biagio. "And I've come all the way from my warm home in Florence to help you with this little book of yours, and I stayed up half the night listening to you explain it to me, and was awakened frightfully early so that you could—"

Niccolò released his grip on Biagio's hand. Biagio popped the cheese into his mouth without even bothering to finish his sentence, bringing an instant smile to Niccolò's lips.

"We've been friends a long time," Niccolò said, reaching down to pick up the last slice of finocchiona. "Good friends."

"Except for when you came back from Forlì without a portrait of Lady Caterina," quipped Biagio. "On second thought, I don't believe I should pay the bill." Niccolò's spontaneous laughter encouraged Biagio to keep poking fun at him. "I must say, that part in your little book about a prince having to learn how not to be good in order to succeed fits you rather well."

By the look on Niccolò's face, Biagio couldn't tell whether he appreciated his little jab or not. "No offense, of course," he added rather quickly. "But I'm afraid it's true."

Niccolò laughed. "Actually, not being good comes rather naturally to me," he replied.

"As it did to Cesare Borgia, I take it," said Biagio.

"He used goodness or the lack of it according to the necessity of the case."

"And you don't?"

Niccolò ignored the dig and continued with his commentary. "And although he was considered cruel," he said, "the duke could be judged more merciful than the leaders of Florence whose excess of mercy has allowed disorders to arise, and bloodshed for entire communities. The actions taken by a good prince, on the other hand, cruel as they may be, aim to injure only a few individuals."

"I must say, I agree with the rule you established in the chapter where you ask whether it is better to be loved or feared," said Biagio. He thought for a moment: "Let me see, how does it go? One ought to be both feared and loved, but as it is—"

"—difficult to be both, it is much safer to be feared than loved," Niccolò interjected. "The important thing is not to be hated."

"So you contend that the Duke of Valentino was not hated?" asked Biagio.

"The duke gained the love and respect of his subjects throughout the Romagna despite his cruelty," argued Niccolò. "He directed his ire solely at those advocating revolt and conspiracy, or as in the case of Remirro de Orca, leaders who abused their office and mistreated the people."

Biagio needed no explanation as to whom Niccolò made reference. Remirro de Orca, the duke's strongman overseeing the city of Cesena, was found in the town square one morning in   a pool of his own blood, hacked into two pieces. A knife and a slab of wood used by butchers to split carcasses lay at his side. His body sat on display for days to showcase the duke's ability to strike quickly and effectively, as well as to appease his subjects who were the victims of Remirro's harsh and despotic rule. This spectacle of pure savagery by the duke turned out to be only a preview of the coup de grâce he delivered just a few days later in the city of Senigallia against a band of rebellious military captains.

"I enjoyed reading your account of that episode more than anything in the world," said Biagio. "Except, of course, for your little book," he added, catching himself. "And your *Discourses,* when you finish with it . . . and, it goes without saying, all the letters you wrote during your travels," he teased. Biagio did all he could to hold back a snicker, especially after noting that Niccolò's lips had parted into a wide smile.

"And my story of Lucrezia," said Niccolò. "The most amusing comedy you'll ever see."

"Lucrezia? La Riccia?" said Biagio, a tad puzzled. "You've written a play about La Riccia?"

"Not yet, but I will. The story and its characters have been floating around in my head for some time now, and your falling in love with our dear Lucrezia has given me an idea," said Niccolò, more than just a little excited.

"Glad I could be of help," quipped Biagio. "I don't see how it could be more entertaining than the murderous love affair you described between the Duke of Valentino and the Orsini family, however."

Biagio went on to talk about Niccolò's second visit with Cesare Borgia in the city of Imola. Despite having just lost the city of Urbino, and having his closest allies bent on overthrowing him, the duke's mood was quite a bit more accommodating than during their previous encounter a few months earlier. Paolo and Giambattista Orsini, together with five other captains— Oliverotto da Fermo, Vitellozzo Vitelli, Giampaolo Baglioni, and two representatives for the dethroned rulers of Urbino and Siena—signed a pact near Lake Trasimeno to thwart the duke's advances in the Romagna.

"How the duke could have remained so confident while completely surrounded by enemies is still a mystery to me," said Biagio.

"The solution he had planned for them was more severe and irrevocable than anything they could have ever imagined," replied Niccolò. "His isolation, in fact, allowed him to act quickly, decisively, and in total secret; the support of his father in the Vatican and the promise of troops from the King of France bolstered his self-assurance; and, finally, he considered them all a band of losers. He derived his confidence from all those factors. He told me as much privately."

While in that same private conversation, the duke showed Niccolò a letter from the King of France promising to send three hundred lancers to aid him in his conquests. Niccolò knew right there and then, from the way the duke carried himself and the strength of his convictions, that he would be victorious over his enemies. Many of the ideas that had been brewing inside of Niccolò for years concerning the nature of politics crystallized during those days of intense interaction with the duke. Watching him maneuver with dexterity and ease in such a hostile environment, deploying appropriate measures of forcefulness, cunning, and unpredictability, taught Niccolò much about the nature of a true prince. It was impossible to know what the duke would do next! Niccolò's mind was made up: An alliance with the duke could only bode well for the Republic, especially at a time in which Florence's influence and powers were weakening. He told the Signoria as much that very night in a missive he composed with the enthusiasm of a young boy.

"As much as he revealed to me of the king's support, and of other tricks he had up his sleeve, the duke refused to tell me of his plans for the Orsini, Vitelli, and the rest of his captains," said Niccolò. "All he revealed at first were his well-placed and expertly dissembled gestures of reconciliation toward them."

"Remirro de Orca's hacking in two was exactly that, was it not?" asked Biagio. "A form of reconciliation."

"A savage and brilliant move," said Niccolò. "Since the Orsini directed the blame to Remirro for the revolt of Urbino, the duke saw an opportunity to placate the people of Cesena, who despised Remirro's tyranny, and at the same time, lure his enemies into believing he had sided with them. He even sent away the French troops that were under his command as a sign of appeasement."

What further impressed Niccolò was the duke's insistence on pursuing a scheme of outwitting and deceiving the gang of conspirators rather than simply overpowering them, even though he felt sufficiently armed to take out his vengeance at any time. The duke continued to play the fox by promising not to injure Giovanni Bentivoglio of Bologna. A ransom of four thousand ducats sealed the peace between them. In return, they restored the city of Urbino to the duke and promised never to ally themselves or go to war with anyone without his assent. And together, the duke and his former henchmen agreed they would march on the city of Senigallia.

"It was here that the fox lured this pride of lions into a trap," said Niccolò.

Niccolò explained to Biagio that the city of Senigallia

surrendered shortly afterward, but the castellan of the fortress refused to capitulate to anyone other than to Cesare Borgia, who once again saw an opportunity for deception. He persuaded the Orsini and Vitelli to wait for him there while he departed for the nearby city of Fano, where he shared his scheme with eight of his trusted allies. He ordered them to meet the Orsini brothers, Vitellozzo Vitelli, and Oliverotto da Fermo on the outskirts of Senigallia, and accompany them into the city on his behalf. The duke, meanwhile, assembled an army of two thousand cavalrymen and ten thousand foot soldiers to march with him to Senigallia.

"Vitelli and the Orsini were completely fooled by the duke's actions," said Niccolò. "After all, it was the castellan who asked them to come into the city. No one suspected a thing."

"I find it amazing that Vitellozzo Vitelli fell into the duke's net so easily," said Biagio. "He should have known better than anyone not to trust a prince you have wronged in the past."

"Once again, the duke thought of everything," Niccolò said. "Vitellozzo was wary at first, but Paolo Orsini, whom the duke had corrupted with all sorts of promises and gifts, finally convinced him there was no need to worry."

Niccolò continued the story: Once the Orsini and Vitellozzo Vitelli arrived in Senigallia, they immediately set out to meet the duke, who was approaching the city with his troops from along the riverbank, descending in from the mountains. Oliverotto remained in Senigallia with a small band of infantry and horsemen. They all entered the city, dismounted at the duke's quarters, and followed him into his private chambers, where they no doubt expected to celebrate their latest conquest. Instead, they were seized and thrown into prison, while outside the duke's troops rapidly carried out their orders of subduing and disarming Oliverotto's men. Vitellozzo and Oliverotto were strangled to death that very night, and the Orsini brothers met the same fate shortly afterward. The duke's intricate and expertly detailed plan had been executed to perfection.

Although Biagio had read the account of this incident countless times, he listened to Niccolò's retelling of it as if it were a bedtime story. To Niccolò, however, the duke's handling of the entire event served as present-day proof that the precepts he laid out in his little book were based on seeing what he called "the truth of the matter" rather than relying on imagination or fantasy.

A thimbleful of wine still sat at the bottom of Niccolò's cup. He gulped it down, wiped his lips with the back of his hand, and stared straight into Biagio's eyes.

"The duke summoned me into his quarters that night," he said. "His face beamed with what could only be called pure exhilaration. He then told me what he had just done, and boasted that he'd been planning his revenge since the last time we met in Urbino, months ago, and that he had done himself, and our Republic, a great favor." Niccolò cleared his throat, determined to make his point once again: "If only those petty henchmen had been the leaders of Italy's perennial invaders from across the Alps," he declared, "France, Spain, or the Hapsburgs of the Holy Roman Empire, the peninsula would be well on its way toward peace."

Both men fell silent. The truth of Niccolò's last words hung in the air. *Niccolò's little book could indeed save us,* thought Biagio to himself, *were anyone of virtue to truly understand its meaning.*

Niccolò took a deep breath and began reciting from his little book as if he were proclaiming a sacred truth: "Whoever, therefore, finds it necessary in his new principality to protect himself against enemies, to gain friends, or conquer land by force or fraud; to be loved and feared by his people, and revered by his soldiers; or finds it necessary to eliminate those who can do him injury, or must introduce innovations into old customs, and be severe as well as kind, and magnanimous as well as liberal; or must suppress a disloyal militia and create a new one, or maintain the friendship of kings and princes, there can be no better example to follow than the actions of this man."

More than hang on Niccolò's words, or derive inspiration from them, Biagio found himself concentrating on the man himself. What he saw, perhaps for the first time, was a dear friend, an emerging author and political thinker, forced to delve back into his past to find inspiration while having to fight off the melancholy and nostalgia that accompanied it. He saw a man whose glory days lay behind him, yet who desperately sought the opportunity to shape a better future for himself; a man who couldn't simply wait for that opportunity to present itself, but felt compelled to create it. *The Prince* was that opportunity. It represented his willingness to adjust to the changing winds of time, mold Fortune to his needs, and plow ahead. Every ounce of insight acquired from a lifetime of study, and fourteen strenuous years of practical experience, went into each principle he put forward in that book. All his hopes and expectations for a dignified reentry into Florence as a respected citizen poured into each word. He wrote the truth as he saw it, and as no one else before had ever seen it, or had the audacity and courage to express it. Biagio was never more proud of his old friend than he was at that moment.

The twinkle in Biagio's eye piqued Niccolò's curiosity.

"So, after a full night and a good part of the morning discussing my little book, it appears you still have more to say?" asked Niccolò.

"I've changed my mind," said Biagio, arousing Niccolò's curiosity further. "I believe I should pay the bill."

Chapter Fifteen

1512: THE FALL OF THE REPUBLIC

In the ten years that followed the momentous meeting with Cesare Borgia, Niccolò became even more useful to the Republic, and virtually indispensable for its foreign relations. The added value he provided to the position of the Second Chancery became the expected standard, and the Signoria's dependence on his sage, detailed, and well-informed political analysis grew stronger by the day. Francesco Soderini's brother, Piero, who had become chancellor for life in 1502, relied on Niccolò for all of Florence's most sensitive missions. But as the years went by, the inevitable winds of change began to take hold. By 1511 Pope Julius II's on-again-off-again relationship with France had reached its limit. The French had to go. The pope formed a Holy League together with King Ferdinand of Spain, the Duke of Ferrara, the Republic of Venice, King Henry VIII of England, and Emperor Maximilian. Their aim was to rid Italy of the French forever. Being a longtime ally of France, Florence found itself isolated.

Despite the overwhelming military superiority of the French, and their victories against Spanish troops in Brescia and the surrounding areas, Louis XII recalled his army back to France, apparently spooked by the entrance of the revered Swiss army onto the battlefield against them. Not long afterward, the cities of Bologna, Parma, Piacenza, and Milan fell under the pope's control, leaving Florence the lone survivor, and completely surrounded. By late summer of 1512, Spanish troops had set up camp near the city of Prato, about a day's march from Florence's city walls. The commander of the Spanish forces—which, after a series of hard-fought battles, were beleaguered and undernourished—offered Florence several options to avoid a frontal attack, including the dismissal of Piero Soderini as its gonfalonier and the reentry of the Medici as its rulers. The Great Council, however, rejected all their demands, hoping to negotiate a better deal. But given the desperate state of the Spanish troops, this turned out to be a serious miscalculation. The unruly Spanish troops, blinded by their hunger and pent-up rage, pummeled the walls of the city until a breach was opened. They entered Prato and laid waste to it, looting, raping, and killing everyone in sight. More than four thousand citizens died that day.

The news of the sack of Prato sent the inhabitants of Florence into a panicked frenzy. Members of the city's elite and sympathizers of the Medici stormed the Palazzo Vecchio demanding Soderini's removal. Realizing there was nothing more that could be done, Niccolò and his colleague in the Chancery, Francesco Vettori, accompanied Soderini from the building and escorted him home. That same evening, Soderini abandoned Florence for the city of Siena. The assault on the Palazzo Vecchio and the exile of Florence's ruler left a permanent scar on the Republic, and led to its ultimate death.

The Medici wasted no time cleaning house. They disassembled the parts of the Signoria they found burdensome, and reestablished the Balía, which essentially did their bidding. Civil servants loyal to Soderini were summarily fired. Despite being a staunch advocate of the republican form of government, Niccolò held out some hope of retaining his job. Wanting desperately to be of assistance to his beloved city during this difficult transition, he offered the new rulers the only thing he had to give: his political expertise.

Their answer came in a series of increasingly harsh rebukes. The first was an outright dismissal from his post. A few days later he was ordered to pay one thousand florins as a form of security restricting him to remain within the borders of the Florentine territories for one year, and next, seemingly out of spite, they prohibited him from entering the Palazzo Vecchio. Niccolò was devastated. To add insult to injury, the Signoria accused him of malfeasance, alleging that he'd pocketed massive sums of money while managing the Florentine militia, which he had initiated, organized, and commanded for the last five years.

This was the last straw for Niccolò. In less than a month's time he'd been humiliated by many of the same people who worked with him in the Chancery, and robbed of all his dignity and respect. As they most likely suspected, knowing Niccolò as they did, no evidence of malfeasance was discovered. He was exonerated completely, but not before his name and reputation were dragged through the mud.

In the aftermath of all the confusion and utter humiliation, Niccolò found himself alone and utterly lost. He languished for hours on end in the room his father had converted into a library when he was still a child, often doing nothing more than staring idly out the window. Books covered nearly every inch of space along the room's four walls, but he couldn't keep his mind on anything long enough to settle into his *sedia Dantesca* and read any of them. Suddenly a man who had made his living, and acquired a certain amount of distinction, by divining future moves on the geopolitical chessboard couldn't see past tomorrow in his own life. Without a steady income, the question of funds became a household issue. Having been a spendthrift his whole life, he felt that abruptly having to rein in his expenses, and even sacrifice a meal or two to pay his debts, was the worst cut of all. And there were four young mouths to feed as well. Marietta, as always, was very supportive. She learned how to stretch out a pot of minestrone, a freshly slaughtered capon, or a meager loaf of bread for days on end.

He'd written letters to friends and ex-colleagues, and even to some within the new administration, offering up his expertise in hopes of securing a position, no matter how small or menial. As the days passed, however, he grew more resigned to his fate. At times, his concentration would return for short spells. Hours once squandered away staring at the walls or worrying about the future were spent reading and "communing with the ancients," as he liked to call it. Since he'd been stripped of everything he'd ever worked for, everything he'd ever wanted, it was all he could do to remain sane. He especially found comfort in the sonnets of Petrarch. He plowed through them, trying desperately to feel something besides anger and resentment. The *Inferno* of Dante also gave him solace, as did the books of his old friends, Livy and Lucretius. But more often than not, he ended up throwing his book down, jumping to his feet, and pacing the floor. Peering out the window onto the busy street just off via Guicciardini, watching the world pass him by, only made matters worse. What was he to do with himself? How would he and his family survive with no income and few savings to sustain them? How could he ever look his neighbors in the eye again?

A few weeks passed and still no response to his letters. Niccolò, as usual, sat in his library, books piled up on his desk, half-written letters scattered everywhere. He perused his bookshelves from his chair, not even bothering to get up. He needed desperately to find some ancient words to soothe him. But nothing seemed to fit the bill. Just then, Marietta called out to him from the kitchen, telling him that the minestrone for the midday meal was nearly ready. Feeling weak, lightheaded, and hungry, Niccolò shuffled into the dining room. At the same time, there was a knock at the door. Marietta hurried out of the kitchen and into the hallway to answer it.

"You just sit down and eat," she shouted to her husband, "and let me give whomever dares interrupt our meal a piece of my mind!"

Niccolò knew she would, so he didn't budge.

When she opened the door, she was met by two burly young men clothed in military garb. Both stood upright, stone-faced, devoid of any expression that would signal the reason for their visit. Naturally frightened, she recoiled, taking a few steps back to better assess the situation. Niccolò didn't have a clear view of the door, but noticed the back of her housedress in the hallway.

"What is it?" he called out.

She said nothing. It was then that the seedier of the two men stepped forward and across the threshold. The other followed.

"What is it you want here?" cried Marietta.

This alarmed Niccolò, who leaped to his feet and raced to meet her. By then, the two men had taken their position just inside the hallway. Their faces came to life when Niccolò appeared behind Marietta. Their eyes locked. Niccolò quickly discerned by their uniforms that they were guards sent by the Balía of Eight.

The seedier guard spoke first: "Signor Niccolò Machiavelli?"

Marietta reached out to grab Niccolò's arm. She clung to it more out of protection for her husband than out of alarm for herself.

Niccolò held her tightly as he answered the man: "What do you want?"

"You are to come with us," said the second man in a voice that commanded obedience.

"What have I done? What is the meaning of this?" Niccolò shot back. "I intend to go nowhere until you explain yourselves."

The two men lunged forward. Marietta tried to stop them, but she and Niccolò could not match their strength. After a moment's resistance, Niccolò's body went slack, surrendering to the inevitable. Marietta cried desperately as they carted him out the door.

The two men led Niccolò at knifepoint down the crowded streets of the city. He lowered his gaze in shame each time he caught the eye of an ex-colleague, longtime neighbor, shopkeeper, or old friend. The humiliation he suffered as he passed the Palazzo Vecchio was particularly difficult to swallow. His feelings of indignity and dishonor came to an abrupt end, however, when he reached the Bargello and its huge doors closed behind him. He knew from experience that once men passed through those gates, they rarely came out alive. But somehow, oddly, he was comforted by the thought. He hadn't experienced that level of calm in weeks. He suddenly felt faint; the world started spinning. His knees weakened and his mind drifted further and further away. Memories of past missions began running roughshod through his head: Julius II, Maximilian of Hapsburg, Louis XII, the faces of their advisors, courtiers, the bishops and cardinals who did their bidding, the *condottieri*, and all the common people who filled the marketplaces and piazzas along the way. They all showed themselves to him as if in a vision. Julius II's long, drawn-out face and dark, solemn expression appeared to him; he sat, dumbstruck, as Niccolò vehemently disputed his plan to bring Bologna and Perugia under papal command, and eventually the Republic of Florence itself. As that image melted away into the ether, it was replaced by Emperor Maximilian's warm, innocent eyes. The poor, inept, but ultimately quite gracious ruler was discussing the pros and cons of invading Florence with a rather bemused Niccolò. It seems he intended to ask the Republic for money to fill his empty coffers before marching into Rome, where he planned to crown himself Holy Roman Emperor.

"What do you find so comical?" a voice rang out.

Niccolò's eyes sprang open. He shook the image of Emperor Maximilian from his brain and the smile from his lips. All he could see now was the flickering of a candle. It illuminated the face of a large, muscular man, his gaze cutting right through him. As Niccolò's eyes slowly adjusted to the darkness, he could make out the sewer rats the size of house cats running freely and the faint silhouette of prison bars several meters off. He suddenly realized he was standing in the middle of a dark, windowless chamber. His arms were tied behind his back. Cries of agony, far-off pleas of men being tortured, or left to die in pools of their own blood, made it nearly impossible to concentrate.

"What do you find so comical?" shouted the large, muscular man standing in front of him.

Niccolò noticed a second man emerge from out of the darkness. The man fastened the rope that held his wrists behind his back to a chain hanging from the ceiling.

"What have I done? What do you want from me?" cried Niccolò.

The second man pulled the chain taut, lifting Niccolò's arms ever so slightly and quite unnaturally upward, just enough to send quivers of pain throughout his whole torso. Niccolò detected a smile on the large man's lips before he spoke: "That is exactly what I'd like to ask you, Signor Machiavelli. What the devil have you done?"

Niccolò, of course, had no answer. The large man persisted. He continued to speak in vague terms about seemingly random events and people, and each time that Niccolò expressed ignorance or incomprehension, the chain was pulled yet another centimeter or two higher. The pain, however, grew exponentially.

Finally, the large man got down to the actual business at hand. "When is the last time you spoke to Agostino Capponi?" he asked.

"I have never heard the name," said Niccolò between moans.

"And Pietro Paolo Boscoli? Are you to tell me you don't know him, either?"

Niccolò said nothing. The chain rose another centimeter. Niccolò howled in agony. "I have no reason to lie to you!" he growled.

"Giovanni Folchi? Niccolò Valori?" shouted the man.

"I don't know them!" Niccolò shot back. "Go to hell!"

As expected, the chain rose again.

"Now answer with the truth, and you can return to your wife and children."

"Go to hell, I said!"

Off in the corner of the cell, the second man grabbed a cast iron handle fastened to a winch and began cranking it, reeling in the chain and lifting Niccolò completely off the ground. His screams echoed throughout the chamber, then quickly stopped, replaced by deep, semi-conscious groans until he went completely silent and passed out cold. The winch was released, allowing Niccolò to free-fall to the stone floor. The second man unhitched the chain from his wrists, and together with the large man, they exited the cell, leaving Niccolò unconscious on the ground.

It wasn't until they had submitted Niccolò to the pangs of the *strappado* four more times that they even bothered to explain what he had been accused of. Each time Niccolò's arms were savagely dislocated from his shoulders, and each time they pulled, twisted, and wrenched them back into their sockets. His interrogators were waiting in vain to hear him admit that he'd conspired to overthrow the Medici regime along with Capponi, Boscoli, Valori, and Folchi, who had already admitted their guilt. Niccolò's name was found scratched on a piece of paper with a dozen other potential sympathizers to the rebel cause. Each and every one of the dozen people on the list were rounded up and tortured. One false or misleading word from any of the plot's hapless ringleaders, or anyone else, would have condemned Niccolò to a lifetime of imprisonment at best, and the hangman's noose at worst.

Niccolò stood before his interrogator a sixth time. After several months of imprisonment and torture he had hardened to their brutality and scorned their ignorance. He told them everything he knew, which was nothing, and still they insisted.

"I believe you are certain of my innocence, but derive satisfaction from torturing me," he said with a smirk pasted on his face.

Sadly, he was absolutely correct. The four ringleaders had admitted weeks ago that they had never spoken to Niccolò about the conspiracy, and in fact, they conceded that they'd never even met him. Their testimonies were borne out, and Niccolò's innocence was firmly established, but the interrogator couldn't resist one last stab at condemning a supporter of "the people" to death. After all, he'd seen many other innocent people confess their guilt after weeks on the rack. Niccolò, however, was not at all like them.

As luck would have it, Giovanni de' Medici was elected pope on the ninth of March, 1513, giving the city of Florence an extra boost of confidence and support. With that confidence came the freedom to show mercy and compassion without being labeled weak or irresolute. Four days later, Giovanni de' Medici, who had taken the name of Pope Leo X, pardoned Niccolò.

Niccolò walked through the gates of the Bargello onto the city streets that very day, and Biagio was right there waiting for him. The second they saw each other, they locked into a firm embrace. It was the first time Biagio had ever seen Niccolò weep.

Chapter Sixteen

1513 – 1527: THE FINAL YEARS

It wasn't enough that the Republic had been replaced with tyranny, and that Niccolò's position at the Second Chancery vanished out from under him; or that he'd been labeled an embezzler and conspirator worthy of imprisonment and the brutality of the *strappado*, and that exile from his native city would become his family's only chance of survival. The final straw came when *The Prince*, the book into which he had poured his heart and soul, was shunned and completely ignored within the new regime. So it was clear that either Francesco Vettori, his friend and ex-colleague, had failed to circulate it within the papal court in Rome or it was simply discarded. Niccolò had dedicated the book to Lorenzo de' Medici, and managed to exploit several of his inside channels to make sure it was delivered to him, but no response ever came. Any hope of finding employment, no matter how meager, within the new government or gaining reentry into Florentine society seemed dashed.

In the years that followed, Niccolò immersed himself in his

Discourses. It became a true labor of love. Divided into three books and numbering 142 chapters of considerable length, the manuscript consumed him. He thought of nothing else day and night but how to form the perfect republic. The farm at Sant'Andrea required increasing amounts of attention, and his issues with money remained the constant anchor around his neck. In the evening, however, when he entered his study and inhabited the world of the ancients, and explored every aspect of their democratic self-rule, every nuance of it, he would breathe the fresh air of freedom.

But still, it was *The Prince* upon which he had placed his bet for a new life—or, rather, a return to his old one. He thought he had bookended his treatise perfectly, penning a carefully worded encomium to Lorenzo de' Medici at the very beginning, and a rabble-rousing paean to freedom and redemption at the end. "An Exhortation to Liberate Italy from the Barbarians" read the twenty-sixth and very last chapter. In it he showered praise upon the Medici, proclaiming that the time was right for a wise and virtuous ruler to introduce a new order of things. *"It would do honor to him and to the people of this country,"* he wrote, proposing the Medici as Italy's new redeemers.

"Italy has been left lifeless," he murmured to himself over and over again, his anger rising as he wrote the chapter. Outrage and zeal fueled his militant mind, and a lasting devotion to the cause of liberation emboldened his pen to craft an emotional call to arms. *"Italy waits for him who shall heal her wounds and put an end to the devastation and plundering of Lombardy, as well as the thievery and taxation suffered by the Kingdom of Naples and Tuscany,"* he wrote.

~

It had been four years since Biagio reviewed, and ultimately transcribed, *The Prince* at the Albergaccio, and today, after not having been in contact for months, he and Niccolò sat across from one another under a wisteria-laden arbor to shade them from the summer sun. Niccolò had just finished writing his exhortation and planned on celebrating it, among other things, with a coterie of friends and fellow Florentines. A festive afternoon banquet was underway, and of course *The Prince*'s exhortation was the topic of discussion. Since late spring of that year, Niccolò had been frequenting the palace of Bernardo Rucellai, a wealthy Florentine who had purchased a vast expanse of fertile land behind the Church of Santa Maria Novella on which he'd built a lavish palace. Highly cultured men from Florence's most influential families gathered periodically in its gardens, known as the Orti Oricellari, to discuss poetry, art, philosophy, history, and whatever struck their fancy. The state of affairs in Italy, and in Florence in particular, always ranked high on their list.

Among this group of distinguished men were Zanobi Buondelmonti and Cosimo Rucellai, to whom Niccolò had dedicated his *Discourses*. Rucellai had been hosting these events since the death of his uncle, Bernardo, the previous year. Others in the group were the acclaimed poet Luigi Alamanni, Antonio Brucioli, Iacopo da Diacceto, Battista della Palla, and the noted philosopher Francesco da Diacceto. Biagio was not a regular visitor to the gardens, but Niccolò had brought him along on this particular day to discuss a subject that had been brewing in his subconscious for some time. And besides, Niccolò knew how much his dear friend enjoyed a good meal. But before Niccolò could guide the conversation in his intended direction, a dispute erupted over the Medici, Florence, Italy, and *The Prince*'s provocative exhortation.

"Do you really think we Italians can match the powers of France, Spain, or even the Germans, as you say in your book?" said Alamanni.

"We have no great armies, it is true, or valorous leaders," said Niccolò, "but if you consider how we perform in duels and hand-to-hand combat, you will see that we Italians, as individuals, surpass all others in strength, dexterity, and style."

"I believe the metaphor you use in your exhortation states it quite eloquently," said Rucellai. "There is great valor in the limbs, but it is lacking in the head."

"No truer words have ever been spoken; we Italians are most definitely lacking in the head," quipped Biagio, forcing a smile to everyone's lips, except for Niccolò, who burst out laughing.

The frequenters of the Orti Oricellari were young, impressionable men, and despite being of aristocratic standing, they felt Niccolò's words on the superiority of the common people resonated with them. Niccolò's personal dream of influencing Florentine politics may have been growing dimmer by the day, but he saw great potential in these men, and they regarded him as a mentor of sorts. Of course, it worked both ways: Their youthfulness invigorated him and rejuvenated the nimbleness of mind that he had lost in last few years of depression and despair. There was still no pulling the wool over his eyes as to the ways of the world, however. He simply saw things from a different perspective now. His point of view had widened. If he once experienced the world as solely tragic, he now also viewed it through the lens of laughter and comedy. *There seems to be no shortage of absurdity in what we deem so solemn,* he reasoned. He came to realize that reality could quite easily be flipped on its head and still hold true. The aspect he cherished most about humor, and always had, was its subversive quality, its ability to attack you unawares. *If gravitas is the lion of politics,* he thought, *then laughter must be the fox.*

"Enough of this talk of republics, tyrannies, and the like," said Niccolò, cutting into the heated debate. "I have invited my dear friend here today to share with him what I have been sharing with all of you." He pulled a small notebook from his satchel, opened it, and began reading: "Our comedy is named for the mandrake root. You'll see the reason as we play it. For you, dear public, I opine, its author has no great repute. But if you don't laugh while we perform it, he'll treat you to a flask of wine."

"A wretched youth will weep and whine," recited Rucellai.

"A doltish man of law will bumble," said Alamanni.

"A venal monk will help him stumble," read Brucioli, glancing down at a slip of paper.

"And a most ingenious parasite will guide them all for your delight," added Francesco da Diacceto.

Everyone broke into spontaneous laughter. They stood up from the table and applauded as Niccolò affected a clownish bow. Biagio clapped along, but still hadn't the slightest idea what was going on. Noticing his friend's confusion, Niccolò gestured for everyone to calm down, which had them all applauding even louder. Rucellai lifted his glass and held it high in the air. The others followed suit.

"Hear, hear," Rucellai toasted, and they all instantly emptied their glasses.

Taking advantage of the moment of silence as they all drank, Niccolò turned to Biagio. "What I have shared with them in these last few months, my dear old friend, is what I have also shared with you for the last few years, and is the centerpiece of my little comedy."

"I don't remember sharing a monk, man of law, or a parasite with anyone, Machia my friend," said Biagio.

"But there is something we do share, or I should say 'someone,' and a beautiful someone at that," Niccolò whispered with a sly grin.

That same sly grin crept onto Biagio's lips. By now Rucellai had refilled everyone's glasses with his vintage Chianti.

"To Lucrezia," said Rucellai.

"To *The Mandrake Root*!" cried Francesco da Diacceto.

"The finest comedy ever written," toasted Alamanni.

And once again, everyone downed their glasses in one gulp.

Of course, Niccolò hadn't yet finished the play. In fact, he'd only written the prologue, but he and the young men of the Orti Oricellari had been discussing it for months. The inspiration Niccolò drew from his talks with Biagio and his young protégés proved invaluable. The idea of a Florentine crafting a play to rival the master works of Ludovico Ariosto in Ferrara and La Bibbiena in Urbino excited his young friends to no end.

Eventually, the story of the wretched swain who desired Lucrezia, the famously beautiful and incorruptible wife of a simple-minded doctor, went on to be performed in the gardens of the Orti Oricellari to great acclaim. Niccolò wrote and rewrote *The Mandrake Root* for each new venue that came along, whether it was Rome, Venice, or his beloved Florence. What he soon realized, and what intrigued Niccolò perhaps more than anything else, was how, in one form or another, all the characters in his play were actually a part of him: Callimaco, the unrelenting youth who lived for love; Nicia, the bumbling academic well past his prime; and Ligurio, the mischievous ruffian, capable of finding his way in and around everything.

Producing literature intended not only for princes and heads of state, but also for anyone willing to laugh at life's absurdities, provided Niccolò with a true sense of fulfillment; creating literary works designed to entertain as well as educate filled him with pure joy. Of course, Niccolò being Niccolò, entertainment felt devilishly similar to education. During these few years, he also penned short stories, poems, and other comedies, each satirizing social norms, the political status quo, or the Church of Rome—and, in the case of *The Mandrake Root,* all three.

The success of his "lighter" works opened doors for Niccolò that had previously been slammed shut. His bond with the members of the Orti Oricellari brought him into Cardinal Giulio de' Medici's good graces and helped rectify some of the damage that had been done to his name and reputation. The group's connections with the cardinal, who had taken over the reins of government after Lorenzo's death in 1519, had always provided a ray of hope for Niccolò. To demonstrate his skills as a historian and storyteller, he even dedicated an oration to the members of the group entitled *The Life of Castruccio Castracani,* about a *condottiere* of humble birth who by dint of his innate Virtue attained great success and ultimately became a prince. This led to a commission in 1520 to write a book, *Histories of Florence,* funded by Cardinal Giulio de' Medici and Pope Leo X himself. Nine months later, his book *The Art of War* went into print. Biagio, as always, was at Niccolò's side and provided a helping hand during the creation of that work. At fifty-one years of age, eight years after his ignominious departure from his native Florence, Niccolò was finally receiving the scholarly and financial recognition he deserved.

Fortune, as always, would present its challenges for Niccolò in the days to come. His enthusiasm for the group at the Orti Oricellari proved so strong, their respect for him so intoxicating, and his lectures on the benefits of a free republic so inspirational that matters soon spiraled out of control. Banishment and death would once again shake the very ground beneath Niccolò's feet. Shortly after Niccolò received his commission to pen his *Histories of Florence,* Cardinal de' Medici floated a plan to restore the former Florentine Republic. When hopes for its implementation dimmed and ultimately died, the members of the Orti Oricellari, being young, ambitious, enterprising, and eager to leave their mark on history, devised a plot to assassinate the cardinal, bring back the Great Council, and restore the government to the people. Apparently, Niccolò's words of caution and outright condemnation of conspiracies were outweighed by his vilification of tyranny.

Before the plot would ever come to fruition, however, a courier carrying dispatches relating incriminating details was captured. He confessed to having spoken with Iacopo da Diacceto, who was quickly rounded up, thrown into prison, and tortured until he finally admitted his guilt. They arrested Luigi Alamanni di Tommaso shortly thereafter. Both men were beheaded for their crime. Buondelmonti and others in the group were more fortunate; they were able to flee the city, and ultimately the country, undetected. Fortunately, Niccolò was spared the ordeal this time around, but without the hope and stimulation of the Orti Oricellari in his life, he once again found himself isolated, alone, and dependent on his writing as his only consolation.

Several years later, in early June of 1527, Niccolò stood along the banks of the Arno observing the steady flow of activity: women slapping their laundry against the rocks at the river's edge; boats docking below the Ponte della Trinita; and feluccas sailing west-ward to the Tyrrhenian Sea. Ever since he had moved back to his beloved city a few years ago, he made sure to take advantage of every moment he could to enjoy its many offerings. Watching its citizens enjoy their hard-earned freedom ranked highest on his list. It had been nearly a month since the Republic was restored to the city once again, ending nearly fifteen years of Medici rule. Word had just gotten out that Niccolò Capponi was elected Gonfaloniere of Justice. Niccolò, on the other hand, hadn't yet heard if his old post as secretary of the Second Chancery would be his. Despite having been in many tight spots during his time as ambassador, he'd never felt quite so anxious as now. He thought back on how cocky he was when Marcello Adriani first offered him the position. He was young and inexperienced back then, but deep down inside, he knew he would get the job. He was now arguably the most qualified person on the continent, and he honestly wasn't sure of his chances.

These were bittersweet days for Niccolò. He had celebrated his fifty-eighth birthday a few weeks earlier, on the third of May, just prior to the fall of the Medici and the reinstallation of the Great Council. The Republic was in full swing. His diplomatic talents were being put to good use as well. Cardinal Giulio de' Medici saw to that when he was elected Pope Clement VII in 1523. Protecting Florence from ruin at the hands of the Holy Roman Emperor, Charles V, became his primary mission. A major war was looming back then that threatened to engulf the entire peninsula, and Niccolò, who, as usual, saw its catastrophic consequences before anyone else, was charged with trying to safeguard the peace. He devised a plan to reinforce Florence's city walls, which impressed both the pope and his lieutenant, Francesco Guicciardini, so much that he was awarded the position of superintendent of the city's fortification system. Indeed, Niccolò had much to celebrate on this particular birthday, especially considering the fact that his efforts went on to prevent a full frontal attack by the invading Imperial forces, and saved the lives of thousands of fellow citizens in the process.

The events that transpired the day following his birthday, the fourth of May, were not as celebratory. Word had reached Florence that Emperor Charles V's troops under the command of the Duke of Bourbon had entered Rome. Two days later, on the sixth of May, they sacked the entire city: Churches, convents, and monasteries were destroyed; palaces of cardinals and other top-ranking members of the Church were looted and burned; the papal guard was decimated; thousands of citizens were killed, and countless women were beaten and raped. The level of brutality and savagery created shockwaves throughout the continent. Niccolò and Francesco Guicciardini hurried down to Rome to negotiate for the pope's safety, resulting in Clement VII's surrender and ultimate freedom, but not without paying a ransom of four hundred thousand ducats to the Imperial forces. The cities of Parma, Modena, and Piacenza as well as the port of Civitavecchia were also handed over to the Holy Roman Empire as part of the deal.

Niccolò returned to Florence a tired and sick man. While in Rome he had begun to experience slight pains in his abdomen, but it didn't worry him much. He chalked it up to enjoying too much good food and wine wherever he went. The doctors prescribed daily doses of aloe to calm the intestinal tract, which seemed to help. As he observed the graceful flow of the riverboats sailing under the Ponte Vecchio, a voice echoed from behind him.

"Mind if I join you?"

Niccolò didn't even bother to turn around, knowing perfectly well who it was.

"Do you bring good news?" Niccolò asked.

"Good news?" said Biagio, pulling up alongside him. "What more could you ask for? Our city is free, unharmed, and as beautiful as ever."

"Our dear country, however, is as much a slave to the will of foreign powers as it has ever been," said Niccolò. "The Holy Roman Emperor and the Spanish rule over us with a firm hand."

"Where is your prince when we need him?" quipped Biagio.

Niccolò said nothing at first. "Once again Fortune has not been our friend, my dear Biagio," he finally uttered. "The Imperial forces were tired, hungry, and short on supplies. Were it not for our usual blundering and indecision, we would have overcome."

"That is not Fortune, Machia my friend," said Biagio. "I believe you would call that a lack of Virtue."

"To be clear, I refer to Giovanni delle Bande Nere," said Niccolò.

"Caterina Sforza's son?" asked Biagio.

"There was no one whom our troops respected more, or produced more fear among our enemies," said Niccolò. "He had all the qualities that I saw in Cesare Borgia. His bravery went unquestioned; he was impetuous, unpredictable, and—"

"And the son of a courageous, impulsive, and temperamental woman!" said Biagio.

"And equally unfortunate, I'm afraid," Niccolò quickly added.

Biagio cast his gaze downward. There was true sadness in his eyes. "He died much too young."

"As did Cesare Borgia," said Niccolò in a near whisper,

"and just as we were beginning to gather around him." Niccolò paused a moment, seemingly too choked up to speak. "Victory would surely have been ours," he finally uttered.

Biagio looked into Niccolò's eyes. *They would share this moment of sorrow,* he thought to himself. *Surely we must not celebrate Florence's good fortune while Italy bleeds,* he wanted to say. He also wanted to convey the news he'd heard from the Palazzo Vecchio, but what he saw in his old friend—his expression, the slight hunch of his shoulders, his pallor, the beads of sweat on his brow—unsettled him.

"Have you eaten today?" Biagio asked.

Niccolò fell silent. He knew what that question really meant. No Florentine would ever ask if you'd eaten unless you looked ill. Food equaled health; there were no two ways about it.

"Let me accompany you home," said Biagio. "A healthy dose of Marietta's vegetable broth should fix you up."

"Ligurio, the parasite in my *Mandrake Root,* could not have thought of a more artful way to invite himself to dinner," said Niccolò, forcing a smile, "and I would enjoy that very much, by the way, but as you can surmise, I am awaiting news from the Palazzo Vecchio."

Biagio affected a smile, too. "Ah, yes, the Palazzo Vecchio. I am sure you have given thought to the fact that for the last several years you have been working for our Medici lords."

"The irony of it has not been lost on me, dear Biagio," said Niccolò, wiping the sweat from his brow. "My intent was to save Florence from destruction, not to preserve Medici rule."

Biagio took a second to compose himself. He made sure to lock eyes with his ailing friend. Niccolò recognized all too well that solemn look on Biagio's face. It was the same expression he wore when he heard news of the Spanish attack on Prato, when Charles VIII marched triumphantly into Florence, and especially when Niccolò returned from Forlì without his much-desired portrait of Caterina Sforza.

"I asked if you bore news for me when you arrived," said Niccolò calmly. "That furrowed brow of yours tells me that perhaps you do."

"And judging from the look of you, I would say it is time to get you home in one piece," said Biagio, obviously dodging the question.

Niccolò didn't budge, and had no intention of going anywhere until Biagio spit out what he knew. He stood firm, weathering the spasms of pain in his abdomen as best he could.

"You told me I would be vilified for my words in *The Prince,* and you were right," he said, "and that the wealthy would never trust me; the poor would see me as a friend to princes and tyrants; and the Church would view me no better than Martin Luther himself."

"And you once told me that just as a prince should not worry about being considered ruthless or cruel in defense of his people, or for the sake of true peace, you do not worry about being despised for revealing the truth of things," said Biagio as he took his friend by the arm. "And now I believe it is truly time for us to go."

Biagio led Niccolò up the slight incline leading to the street, and together they braved the rutted cobblestone to via Guicciardini.

Marietta ran to help Niccolò the moment she saw him and Biagio walk through the door. She took her husband by the arm, and together with Biagio, they walked him to his bed.

"Here, take these," said Marietta, handing Niccolò several tablets of his prescribed remedy.

"Should I fetch him some water?" asked Biagio.

"No need. He prefers a bit of wine to wash them down," answered Marietta, reaching for the half-emptied carafe by the side of the bed.

"Then I will leave you with him," said Biagio, who then turned to his old friend with a smile.

Finding it difficult to speak, Niccolò acknowledged him with a slight nod. Biagio reached out and held his hand, bid him farewell, and ambled out the door.

Marietta slid a chair over and sat with Niccolò all that day, and the next, tending to his every need. The pastilles of aloe, which had succeeded in quelling the bloating of his stomach, and in soothing his pain for the past several weeks, had not produced their desired effects. His condition, in fact, worsened. During his short periods of lucidity, he spoke to Marietta more freely and more openly than he'd ever done before. He regretted not spending enough time with her and asked forgiveness for being gone on missions for such long stretches. Knowing she worried about the children and the future of the household, he reminded her that in his last will and testament, he left everything to his four sons, Ludovico, Bernardo, Piero, and Guido, and for his daughter, Bartolommea, he had secured a dowry.

"And you, my dear dear Marietta, shall execute the will as you see fit," he whispered as tears welled up in his eyes, "and keep guard over the welfare of the children, which you have always done, and for which I can never thank you enough."

On the twenty-second of June, Niccolò agreed it was time to confess his sins. Despite all the invectives he had hurled against the Church throughout his life, calling a priest at a time like this was simply the normal course of action, and certainly raised no eyebrows among those who knew him well.

"My grievances are not with God," he told Marietta, "but with the men of God." He knew that many Florentines at the time felt the same, but few dared to be as candid as Niccolò.

Frá Matteo, the local pastor, was called to the house. Marietta met him at the door.

"If he manages to stay alive throughout his entire confession," she quipped, "and confesses all his sins, it will take so long that he will surely outlive us all."

Niccolò died that very day. He was laid to rest in the family chapel in the Church of Santa Croce. Throngs of friends and family members lined up to pay their respects, each stopping in front of his tomb to say a short prayer.

Biagio, however, stayed a bit longer than the rest to have his final chat with the man he knew and loved for all of his adult life. Everyone had left the church by then. Biagio stood alone, at first saying nothing, just staring at the white marble sarcophagus.

"You once told me of a dream you had," he began, intent on giving his own personal eulogy. "You saw a crowd of hungry and miserable people. When you asked who they were, you were told they were the blessed souls on their way to heaven. Upon seeing a second group of solemn men whom you could distinguish as great philosophers of Greece and Rome, you were told they were the souls condemned to suffer in hell for all eternity."

A devilish smile formed on Biagio's lips as he uttered his next few words: "And when asked with which group you preferred to remain when you died, you said, without question, you would rather be with all those great minds discussing politics."

Biagio stood up straight, and spoke directly and honestly

to his old friend and colleague. "You were never one to tell lies. They did not become you. So I believe you when you say you would prefer the company of great men, and I am sure you are with them right now. But you have also been wrong several times in your life. So allow me to say that you are quite mistaken in this case. You and those great men with whom you now find yourself discussing questions of state are not in hell as you would presume, but undoubtedly in the highest realms of heaven, because, my dear Machia, the Devil would never have you."

Biagio wiped the tears from his eyes, nodded a final farewell to his old friend, and walked off.

Acknowledgments

My interest in Niccolò di Bernardo dei Machiavelli goes way back to my years in graduate school. Guido Guarino, my esteemed professor of humanism and Renaissance at the time, opened my eyes to Machiavelli not only as a groundbreaking political thinker, but also as an accomplished author of plays, satires, and novellas. Professor Guarino's approach to Machiavelli was rigorously objective and straightforward, yet full of passion and humanity. He urged students to dive right into Machiavelli's works, examine them at face value, study each word and clever turn of phrase, and appreciate them as sophisticated political philosophy and as literature to be devoured. I'd have to say that when I sat down to collect my thoughts on how to tackle the biography of such a misunderstood, maligned, and extremely complex man, I found a virtual gold mine in the reams of notes I took during Professor Guarino's information-packed lectures. His Machiavelli was more than an astute and fearless political philosopher; he was a man with a wry sense of humor and a writer of notable substance. My gratitude goes out to Professor Emeritus Guido Guarino for giving me an honest, sober, and penetrating introduction to such a preeminent figure in Italian history.

Writing a compelling account of Machiavelli's life from the point of view of his controversial, and often scorned, political philosophy had its challenges, to say the least. As a necessary first step, I reexamined his two seminal works, *Discourses on the First Decade of Titus Livy* and, of course, *The Prince*. My old dog-eared copy of *Il Principe*, edited by Ugo Dotti, with the myriad handwritten notes I had written in the margins as a grad student, served as my bible of sorts and kept me company throughout the entire composition of this book. Machiavelli's own *Florentine Histories* and Francesco Guicciardini's *The History of Italy* provided much of the historical backdrop I needed, while Professor Pasquale Villari's *The Life and Times of Niccolò Machiavelli,* a four-volume, sixteen-hundred-page biography, laid out all the pertinent social, political, historical, and cultural information of the period in meticulous detail, including specifics on Machiavelli's personal and professional history. I referred to noted scholars such as Quentin Skinner and Harvey C. Mansfield for much of my political analysis. Skinner's succinct, lucid, and vastly illuminating book, *Machiavelli,* helped me wade through the political complexities on the Italian peninsula in the late fifteenth and early sixteenth centuries, and Mansfield's dissection of Machiavelli's political principles and philosophy in *Machiavelli's Virtue* added considerable depth to my understanding of the man and his times.

In terms of creating a flesh-and-blood, sympathetic (to a degree), and multidimensional lead character, Machiavelli's numerous letters turned out to be my best resource. His own direct and incisive words went a long way toward painting a picture of an intelligent, no-nonsense man with a scathing wit and genuine enthusiasm for life. *Machiavelli and His Friends,* a compilation of missives to colleagues, friends, and family, edited by James B. Atkinson and David Sices, helped me tremendously in this regard, as did *Machiavelli's Legations,* a selection of letters, collected by G. R. Berridge, composed during Machiavelli's many diplomatic ventures for the Republic of Florence.

It would be nearly impossible to undertake a fictional

account of Machiavelli's life without referring to two illustrious Italian scholars and authors, Roberto Ridolfi and Maurizio Viroli. Ridolfi's voluminous biography *Vita di Niccolò Machiavelli* proved invaluable for its detailed investigation into Machiavelli's personal and professional life, insights into his written works, and clear descriptions of the cutthroat world he lived in. Of course, at the heart of any decent work of fiction there must be an interesting protagonist and a compelling story. In that regard, Viroli's excellent biography *Niccolò's Smile* was a lifesaver. He managed to describe Machiavelli, a figure usually perceived to have the cold, cunning, and manipulative characteristics associated with his political principles, as a three-dimensional man with genuine human feelings, needs, and desires, especially when it came to his love for his native Florence. He told the story of a selfless civil servant and a genuine patriot. *Niccolò's Smile* gave me an honest and highly enlightening path to Machiavelli's soul, and for that I can't thank Professor Viroli enough.

And lastly, I would be remiss if I didn't thank the city of Florence itself. Simply walking its streets, exploring its neighborhoods, and visiting the many churches, museums, and public buildings that inhabit its historic center equipped me with all the inspiration and motivation I could ever hope for. My several trips to Machiavelli's farm in Sant'Andrea in Percussina, fourteen kilometers outside of Florence, were facilitated by Elizabetta Mori of the Albergaccio Restaurant. She graciously showed me around Machiavelli's farmhouse, the surrounding grounds, and the inn where he played cards and exchanged words on a daily basis with the local townspeople. I'm particularly grateful to her for taking me to that part of his grounds where Machiavelli undoubtedly stood during his grueling years of exile, most likely in bittersweet silence, to marvel at the grandeur of Brunelleschi's

Duomo atop the church of Santa Maria del Fiore, a monument that tethers every pure-blooded Florentine to their beloved city. For that one brief moment, while standing in that very spot, I caught a glimpse of the man's hopes, dreams, and ultimate disappointments, and for that I have to say "*grazie infinite.*"

About the Author

Maurizio is an award-winning screenwriter, documentary filmmaker, and educator. Holding both American and Italian citizenship, Maurizio has lived and worked in Italy for the past twenty-three years where as an associate professor at a small liberal arts college in Rome he specialized in Italian theater and film while also teaching courses in scriptwriting and adapting literature to the screen. He started out writing plays immediately upon receiving his M.A. in Italian Studies from Middlebury College. His two full-length Italianate farces, *The Abductors* and *Big Deals*, were produced in Santa Cruz, California, and his one-act play, *Joyride*, found success in San Francisco and New York City. As a screenwriter, five of his feature length scripts have been optioned, three of which were either winners or finalists in prominent screenwriting contests. His crime drama, *Ferryman's Grotto*, set in the hills of central Italy, and his musical drama, *One Night in Asbury Park*, were also honored as quarterfinalists and semifinalists, respectively, in the prestigious Nicholl Fellowship in Screenwriting competition. In addition, Maurizio has co-produced two award winning, short documentaries: *Uno degli Ultimi*, an intimate look into the life of an aging contadino (small farmer) in a dying Italian village, and *Beneath the Underdog*, a heartfelt look at immigration and soccer in today's Italy.

Maurizio now lives in a quaint hilltop village in northern Lazio, just a stone's throw from the Tuscan and Umbrian borders, with his wife of many years. He has finally abandoned academia to live the good life writing screenplays and novels full time.

NOW AVAILABLE FROM THE MENTORIS PROJECT

America's Forgotten Founding Father
A Novel Based on the Life of Filippo Mazzei
by Rosanne Welch

A. P. Giannini—The People's Banker
by Francesca Valente

Building Heaven's Ceiling
A Novel Based on the Life of Filippo Brunelleschi
by Joe Cline

Christopher Columbus: His Life and Discoveries
by Mario Di Giovanni

Dreams of Discovery
A Novel Based on the Life of the Explorer John Cabot
by Jule Selbo

The Faithful
A Novel Based on the Life of Giuseppe Verdi
by Collin Mitchell

Fermi's Gifts
A Novel Based on the Life of Enrico Fermi
by Kate Fuglei

God's Messenger
The Astounding Achievements of Mother Cabrini
A Novel Based on the Life of Mother Frances X. Cabrini
by Nicole Gregory

Grace Notes
A Novel Based on the Life of Henry Mancini
by Stacia Raymond

Harvesting the American Dream
A Novel Based on the Life of Ernest Gallo
by Karen Richardson

Humble Servant of Truth
A Novel Based on the Life of Thomas Aquinas
by Margaret O'Reilly

Leonardo's Secret
A Novel Based on the Life of Leonardo da Vinci
by Peter David Myers

Marconi and His Muses
A Novel Based on the Life of Guglielmo Marconi
by Pamela Winfrey

Saving the Republic
A Novel Based on the Life of Marcus Cicero
by Eric D. Martin

Soldier, Diplomat, Archaeologist
A Novel Based on the Bold Life of Louis Palma di Cesnola
by Peg A. Lamphier

The Soul of a Child
A Novel Based on the Life of Maria Montessori
by Kate Fuglei

FUTURE TITLES FROM THE MENTORIS PROJECT

Cycles of Wealth
Fulfilling the Promise of California
A Novel Based on the Life of Alessandro Volta
A Novel Based on the Life of Amerigo Vespucci
A Novel Based on the Life of Andrea Doria
A Novel Based on the Life of Andrea Palladio
A Novel Based on the Life of Angela Bambace
A Novel Based on the Life of Angelo Dundee
A Novel Based on the Life of Antonin Scalia
A Novel Based on the Life of Antonio Meucci
A Novel Based on the Life of Artemisia Gentileschi
A Novel Based on the Life of Buzzie Bavasi
A Novel Based on the Life of Cesare Becaria
A Novel Based on the Life of Cosimo de' Medici
A Novel Based on the Life of Father Matteo Ricci
A Novel Based on the Life of Federico Fellini
A Novel Based on the Life of Frank Capra
A Novel Based on the Life of Galileo Galilei
A Novel Based on the Life of Giuseppe Garibaldi
A Novel Based on the Life of Guido d'Arezzo

A Novel Based on the Life of Harry Warren
A Novel Based on the Life of Judge John J. Sirica
A Novel Based on the Life of Laura Bassi
A Novel Based on the Life of Leonard Covello
A Novel Based on the Life of Leonardo Fibonacci
A Novel Based on the Life of Luca Pacioli
A Novel Based on the Life of Maria Gaetana Agnesi
A Novel Based on the Life of Mario Andretti
A Novel Based on the Life of Mario Cuomo
A Novel Based on the Life of Peter Rodino
A Novel Based on the Life of Pietro Belluschi
A Novel Based on the Life of Rita Levi-Montalcini
A Novel Based on the Life of Saint Augustine of Hippo
A Novel Based on the Life of Saint Francis of Assisi
A Novel Based on the Life of Scipio Africanus
A Novel Based on the Life of Vince Lombardi

For more information on these titles and
The Mentoris Project, please visit
www.mentorisproject.org.

Printed in Great Britain
by Amazon